POOCHES, PUMPKINS, AND POISON

A POOCH PARTY COZY MYSTERY

CAROLYN RIDDER ASPENSON

MAGNUM GRACE PUBLISHING

CREDITS

Cover Design by Carolyn Ridder Aspenson

This is a work of fiction. Names, characters, places, brands, media, and incidents are either the product of the author's imagination or are used fictitiously. Any resemblance to similarly named places or to persons living or deceased is unintentional.

CAROLYN RIDDER ASPENSON

COPYRIGHT INFORMATION:
This work is licensed under a Creative Commons Attribution-Noncommercial-No Derivative Works 3.0 Unported License.
Attribution — You must attribute the work in the manner specified by the author or licensor (but not in any way that suggests that they endorse you or your use of the work).
Noncommercial — You may not use this work for commercial purposes.
No Derivative Works — You may not alter, transform, or build upon this work.

For
Brutus, Missy, Bandit, Sam, Max,
Magnum, Gracie, Larka, Capone, and Allie
You're all my favorite dog.

CHAPTER ONE

Most people didn't make a habit of finding dead bodies, but I wasn't most people.

The first body I'd discovered was my husband's, no doubt the most devastating experience of my life. The memory of him lying on our driveway burned in my brain, and it would remain there forever, taunting me, trying desperately to take first place among the twenty-seven years' worth of memories we'd shared. I had yet to let it win, and I promised myself I wouldn't, but there were days that promise weighed heavily on my soul.

The second body I found belonged to the organizer of my town's Halloween Festival, Traci Fielding. I'd found her lying in a pseudo pumpkin patch set up as part of the event. I wasn't at all prepared, but was anyone ever prepared to discover a dead body?

I crouched down close and examined the remains before me, gently placing my fingers against the skin of the dead woman's neck. My lips curled and my stomach performed somersaults in my gut as I got close to her lifeless body, but I persevered. I grimaced at the slight smell of bitter almonds.

I'd never liked almonds, and I'd never understood the love my daughter Hayden had for them.

Traci Fielding had no pulse. I checked her wrist too, just in case I'd missed the right spot on her neck. I'd done the same thing with my husband. My calm surprised me, but I'd promised myself I'd never react the way I had when I'd found Sam on the driveway—panicked, emotional, out of control. It hadn't changed anything. Sam was still dead, and even if I had tried to give him CPR, it wouldn't have helped. He'd suffered a brain aneurysm and died before hitting the ground. I'd lost my husband two years ago. He was fifty-four-years old, and I was only forty-seven. We'd promised to love each other and spend the rest of our lives together. He'd lived up to that promise but unfortunately, I'd only been able to make good on half.

From the looks of Traci Fielding, CPR had no chance of reviving her either. I dug my phone out of my bag and dialed 9-1-1, and then shortly after, things got interesting.

The police arrived within minutes, likely because they were already at the fairgrounds policing the events set up to make sure the townspeople weren't trying to get in prior to the event officially starting. Food trucks were popular in town, and every time we had a festival the lines reached outside the fairgrounds. The actual festival didn't start for days, but that didn't stop people from worming their way onto the grounds to scam samples from the trucks.

A heavy set police officer with beads of sweat covering his face and a quite large receding hairline questioned me. "Did you touch anything, ma'am?"

"Yes, sir. I touched her neck and left wrist checking for a pulse."

"Did you touch any of the pumpkins or anything else?"

"Not that I'm aware of. At least not intentionally."

"How did you come into the area?"

I explained my entrance from the left side.

"And what were you doing here?"

"Just walking around the fairgrounds on my way to the dog area. I run the dogs event. I took a short cut."

"Dogs?"

"I'm with the shelter."

He stared at me like he had no clue what I was talking about. Did he not read the local paper?

"We're bringing dogs here for the kids to play with in hopes someone will want to adopt some."

"Oh, gotcha." He chewed a piece of gum with his mouth open.

I cringed. That was hands down one of my biggest pet peeves. Maybe even my biggest. No, on second thought, talking with a mouth full of food was my biggest. At least in the mouth pet peeves category. I might have had a few more pet peeves than I cared to admit.

"Anyone else here?"

"When I found her?"

"Yes, ma'am."

"Just me."

"See anyone around when you walked up?"

"I wasn't exactly paying attention."

He nodded once. "You think of anything, you let us know, okay?"

"Of course."

He asked for my contact information, and I gave it to him, and then he told me not to tell anyone anything about what I saw, including the victim's name, pointed to our right, and told me how to exit the area.

Mr. Personality.

I coughed. The smell of bitter almond growing stronger and overwhelming my nasal passages. "Do you smell that?"

"Smell what?"

"Almonds?"

He sniffed the air and raised his left brow like I was some kind of crazy person. "All I smell is funnel cake."

"Well, I do, and it's getting stronger, too." I squatted down closer to the area where Traci's body lay and made a circle above the pumpkin next to her. "Right around here."

The officer bent down, smelled it and then quickly backed away, pulling me up in the process. "Ma'am, I'm going to need you to leave immediately."

He called out to another officer and asked for masks and gloves. After he got them, he said, "I need forensics to mark those boot marks over there."

I quickly grabbed my phone and snapped a few photos of the scene, including the prints, though I wasn't sure what compelled me to do that. I did not photograph Traci's body because I just couldn't.

The officer reminded me of his request earlier, but with a stern voice. "Ma'am, you need to back out of this gated area immediately."

A small crowd gathered on the other side of the yellow crime scene tape around the man-made pumpkin patch in the small sodded area of the fairgrounds.

A police officer spoke into a bull horn. "Ladies and gentlemen, the festival area is now closed. We need everyone to immediately exit the fairgrounds in a calm manner. Let me repeat, the festival area is now closed, and this means to vendors, employees, and guests. Everyone must leave immediately."

Gina Palencia, a volunteer for the festival, rushed over to

me. "Missy, I'll walk out with you." She hooked her arm into mine. "I heard someone found a body."

I took in a deep breath and exhaled slowly, doing my best to stay as calm as possible. You can do this, Missy, I thought. You can do this. "It was me. I found the body."

She gasped. "Oh no, are you okay? She guided me over to a row of chairs near the grandstand and into a seat. "What happened?"

"Gina, we have to leave. They just told everyone the festival is closed."

"Oh, yes, right. Silly me. I forgot. You can tell me what happened while we head to the parking lot."

I'd been sternly instructed not to tell anyone about the identity of the victim, and I knew Gina well enough to know she was going to push for the name, so I prepared to keep my lips zipped.

"So, what happened?"

"I'm not allowed to say. They want to notify the family first."

The ambulance drove by.

"Well, I guess we can't see now," she said.

I didn't care to see another dead body ever again.

"Maybe the police chief will have something to say. You want to hang out in the parking lot and wait with me?"

I shook my head. "I've got to get some things done, and besides, I already know what happened, or at least as much as I care to know for now."

As I headed to my car, another volunteer, Jennifer Lee, stopped me. "Missy, do you know what's going on? I heard someone found a dead body?"

I raised my hand. "That would be me."

"Oh my gosh, what happened? Are you okay?"

"I'm fine. I'm sure someone from the police department will need more information from me, but I'm fine."

"What happened?"

"I'm not supposed to say." I smiled. "I'm sorry, but I'm rushing over to the shelter. I'm sure I'll have to address this again soon."

She nodded. "Oh, yes, sure. I'm…I won't keep you. If you need something though, feel free to ask."

"Thanks, Jennifer."

I headed back to the animal shelter to check on the dogs and introduce myself to the new intakes, or newbies as I called them, because there were always newbies. Kerry Pitman, one of our faithful volunteers greeted me by tossing a twenty-five pound bag of kibble at my feet.

She brushed a flyaway strand of her curly strawberry blonde hair from her eyes. "Can you carry that to the back for me? One of the Boy Scout troops donated seventy-five bags this morning, and as usual we're understaffed, so I've been lugging these things in all by myself."

"Seventy-five bags? That's fantastic."

"It is even though my back thinks otherwise."

"I'm sure," I said, lifting the heavy bag over my shoulder and following behind her.

We walked through the kennel area and were greeted by a symphony of barking and howling hellos from the pups. An equal mixture of love and sadness washed over me. I loved each of the dogs like they were my own, and it ripped my heart to pieces because I couldn't find each of them the homes they deserved. We trucked the bags from the front of the shelter to the back of the kennels in no time, but I knew we'd both pay for it later.

Kerry, a few dozen years younger than me, and several dozen pounds heavier, brushed the dust from her hands and sighed. "That's going to hurt tomorrow."

"Tomorrow? I'm thinking later today."

She laughed. "You're probably right. Hey, were you at the fairgrounds when they found the body?"

"Uh," I shrugged my shoulders up toward the sides of my face and cringed. "I'm the one that found the body."

"What? What happened?"

"I'm not allowed to discuss it before the police tell the family."

She rubbed her arm. "Oh, yeah, I get that. Are you okay? Was it weird?"

No one at the shelter knew much about my personal life. They knew my husband had died, and that I'd found him, but I hadn't talked much about our relationship, or the pain I'd gone through since his passing. Our relationship, and the grief I'd experienced, and still experienced every day, was private, and though I shared some of that with Hayden, I kept it hidden from the rest of the world. That and our memories were the only things I had left of us, and I had no intention of sharing any of it with anyone.

"Death is always uncomfortable but it's a part of life."

"Well, sure, but murder isn't."

"What makes you think this person was murdered?"

"Who dies of natural causes in a man-made pumpkin patch at a Halloween festival?"

She agreed. "We may not be that small of a town anymore, but word still travels fast."

I used my personal key to open a locked storage cabinet inside the kennel area and removed a large bag of treats I'd stored inside for the dogs. "True, but trust me, death doesn't check your location before it takes you. When it's your time, it's your time."

"Well, I hope when it's my time, I'm dressed and have my hair done, that's all I have to say about that."

I smiled and headed toward the first kennel with the bag of treats.

Sam worked hard his entire life, and he'd done well for us. We never suffered financially, and because of that, we'd been able to invest our money well. Part of that investment went into retirement funds and a life insurance policy for him. What I didn't know about though, were secret life insurance policies he'd set up for himself in the event that something happened to him. I often wondered if he'd known he would die young, or if he'd simply planned for the possibility. Either way, those extra life insurance policies ended up making me a very wealthy woman.

I didn't need or want that wealth. I wanted Sam, but since I couldn't have him, I put aside enough for Hayden, and did as instructed by my advisors with enough to allow me to live comfortably the rest of my life, or to one hundred. After that there might be an issue, but I doubted I'd live that long. I kept a large sum tucked away in investments and available for emergencies, but I took out a large amount to be able to support the animal shelter and provide for the animals in a way that allowed for a better life in their kennels and cages, and a better chance at a life outside of the shelter. Part of that improvement included treats and toys.

It might sound silly, but treats and toys were rare items in shelters, and they brightened the dogs days. Every little thing counted in my book at least.

"Hey Brutus, what's shaking big guy?" Brutus, a small mixed terrier mutt wagged his little wiry haired nub of a tail as I stuck the treat into his cage and rubbed the top of his head. "You're being a good boy, right?"

"He's always a good boy," Kerry said.

Brutus barked his agreement.

The dogs nearby all waited at the front of their cages for me. I hit each cage or kennel with treats and greeted each dog with a cheery hello and a pat on the head. The newbies stayed in the backs of their kennels, and for those, I gently entered.

We'd only had three newbies since the day before, and for our city, that was a good thing. Being a suburb of Atlanta, we still fell victim to dog fighting that, thanks to a former professional football player and his very public dog fighting crimes, the city was once known for, and Pit Bulls were rampant in town. Pittie support groups had worked hard to curb the fear the dogs were labeled with, and it was working, but there were still too many bully breeds in shelters, and too many bully breed mama's having babies in shelters.

"Hey sweetie." I slid a dog treat across the kennel floor to the blue gray pittie in the cage. "That's for you girl. Go ahead."

She wouldn't make eye contact with me, just stared into the corner of the kennel.

I slid another treat toward her. "How about two? You look like you're hungry, baby."

She slowly moved her head and eyed the treats.

"It's okay. I'll stay over here. I promise."

I watched her little black nose wiggle and she caught a whiff of the bacon scented goodies.

"Go ahead. I hear they're really good, and I've got more if you want them."

She bent her head toward them, took one of the treats in her mouth, and crunched down on it.

"You're a good girl."

She chomped it down quickly and immediately went for the other one. When she finished that one, I slid another one toward her, but not quite all the way. She stared at it.

"It's okay, it's for you, too."

She took two steps toward it, and snatched it up, and gobbled it down.

"There you go. You are hungry, aren't you?" I placed another one on the ground just a foot away from me.

She eyed it, and then finally glanced up at me.

I smiled at her. "It's okay, sweetie. It's okay."

She took another scoot toward the treat.

"Good girl," I said.

"Man that dropped her off said her name is Allie. Said he was allergic. Couldn't keep her."

"Right." Maybe he was, it wasn't my place to judge, and I tried very hard not to. "Allie, get the treat." She raised her eyes to me again, and scooted a little closer. I noticed the white under her chin and wondered how old she was. "It's okay, girl."

She reached out her paw and pushed the treat toward her.

I laughed. "Look at you, being all smart. You're a good girl."

She ate the treat, and I quickly took out another one, but kept it right next to my crossed legs. "Can you do that with this one, too, Allie?"

She barked.

I smiled at her. "Don't you get sassy with me now. Come on, get the treat."

Allie's tail wagged, and she struck a little downward doggie pose.

I didn't move. "Come on Allie. Get your treat."

Whoever had Allie before, whether it was the man who'd just turned her in or someone else, had trained her some, or she was just a really smart dog. She wagged her tail again and stepped closer to me.

"Come on, sweetie. Get your treat."

Allie stretched out her paw and swatted the treat away from my leg, then nabbed it with her mouth and swallowed it down.

Kerry and I both laughed. "That's a good girl," I said. I

took a treat from the bag and held it in my hand. "Here's another one. Come get it."

Allie barked.

"Nope. I'm not going to set it down. You need to come get it."

She barked again.

"I don't care. If you want it, come get it."

She barked again, and I shook my head. It was a battle of wills, but I wouldn't let her win.

Allie took two small, slow steps and then sat in front of me. She didn't touch the treat in my hand, but her tail swept across the floor like a broom. A big pittie smile draped across her face.

"Look at that. You're the flipping dog whisperer," Kerry whispered.

I held out the treat. "Here you go, girl." I gently moved my hand toward her mouth and just slightly under it. When she took the treat, I softly rubbed under her chin, and she laid down, munching on the bone on my legs.

From that moment on, I knew we'd be the best of friends.

I patted her on the head and rubbed her behind the ears. She moaned, and I did then a little, too. It always made me happy to watch a dog relax, to feel them feel loved. It also made my eyes water. For someone that did a bang up job of hiding her true emotions, those darn dogs got me every single time.

I spent thirty minutes in that kennel with Allie, hanging out, giving belly rubs, having a fascinating conversation about politics and religion. Dogs were the only souls other than Sam I talked with about those subjects, and Allie must have been on the same page as me because I received an incredibly unsanitary but satisfying arm bath. When I finally forced myself up from the floor to leave, Allie just casually followed me out and pranced along as I greeted and introduced myself to the other two newbies. We all chatted, shared treats, and all agreed dogs were superior to humans.

My time at the kennel was healing, and I'd completely forgotten I'd found a dead body at the fairgrounds earlier.

A few hours later, Gina called and said they'd cleared the fairgrounds and I could return to continue my set up, so I headed back. I'd grabbed a leash for my new right arm, Allie, and brought her along for the ride. She sat in the car smiling out the window like a princess waving to her people. I couldn't help but laugh at the girl. She found joy in everything she did, and I admired and envied that in her.

I finished setting up the turf and fenced area for the dogs, leaving enough room for ten crates each on the back and right side of the turf. I'd originally planned to bring twenty-five dogs, but with only two additional volunteers committing to helping per shift, decided on just twenty. Ten dogs a person with me overseeing the event was manageable, any more than that might have been too much.

The city had very specific guidelines for the shelter to follow, and since shelter dogs often had unknown pasts, we had to be careful with which dogs we chose to bring as well as keeping a strong eye on all of them.

I'd spent the last two years volunteering for the animal shelter as their canine adoption manager, which, in a nutshell, meant I did everything within my power to make sure the dogs were adopted. I'd come up with the idea to have pooch parties, as I'd called them, adoption events at city sponsored public events that allowed the community to interact with the dogs and show them the animals were adoptable and loving, and worthy of good homes of course.

It had been the most rewarding and heart breaking job I'd ever had, but I'd needed something to do after Sam died. With my daughter Hayden working in Atlanta, I was alone more than I liked, but since I wasn't big on socializing without a reason, and I loved dogs, the shelter work was a perfect fit. Hayden wasn't far from me, but she had her own life and didn't need me or my widowed neediness holding her back from living her dream. And I didn't need to be an emotional widow dependent on her only child to make her feel whole. In fact, I refused to be that person.

Over the past year, I'd worked with a local trainer on collar training and he helped me train the dogs, especially the ones that had been with us the longest. That training had paid off. Those dogs were showed more and were adopted more often than before the training. It was exhausting though, because while I paid for the collars and training with the trainer, he could only train so many dogs. He'd ended up training me to train them, and I became certified and trained other volunteers. I'd spent my free time training the dogs until I had help from volunteers, and still did a lot of it myself. We had over seventy dogs at any given time, not including the fosters, so it was good that I didn't have much of a private life.

I took a break and sat in at the adoption desk I'd set up by the crates. I'd brought a Benebone for Allie and she chewed on it happily by my side. The desk was really just a simple folding table, but it would do the trick.

Since I'd started the pooch parties, we'd adopted out over two hundred dogs with sixty percent of them being older than four, and because of that, we'd received a lot of local press. I'd established a professional friendship with the local newspaper reporter, Jim Decon because of it, and Jim was gracious enough to always give our events top priority both online and in print.

Max Hoover, a local city councilman Sam used to play golf with, introduced us. Max and I had also become sort of friends, though Hayden thought he wanted to be more. He'd recently divorced, and she thought he was interested in me, but I didn't see it. He was a sweet guy, but I'd already found my soulmate, and I didn't see a reason to bother relationshipping with someone else. I didn't think anyone could live up to the standards Sam set, and I saw no reason to even ask them to try. I was grateful for his friendship, though, and I hoped it continued to grow.

Max and Jim opened the small white baby gate I'd put across the turf.

Jim smiled, his big toothy grin stretched the width of his swollen, red face. "Hey there, Missy, word is you're the one that found Traci. Care to chat for a minute?"

I smiled at the men. "I guess they've already released her name?"

They both nodded.

Jim said, "Just a minute ago. Already let Jake know, but that didn't take too long seein' as he was already at the fairgrounds."

Jake was Traci's soon-to-be ex-husband. Their messy divorce had been dragged all over town and made horribly public due to Jake's desire for several local women, plus his inability to keep a specific body part zipped up where it belonged. I wasn't a fan of men that cheated on their wives, and I was less of a fan of men that tried to bully their wives out of what they deserved when said wife busted them for cheating. Traci wasn't the kindest woman in town, and a bit of a control freak, but she didn't deserve to be treated like that. No woman did.

Jake, or Jake Fielding, was a big business man in town with his hands in several companies, mostly restaurants and sports bars across the entire state of Georgia. Sam had once said he was a good business man but had no ethics, and my husband struggled with that. I understood his feeling.

"So, what can you tell me about finding Traci?" he asked.

Max patted my shoulder. "Miss, if you aren't up for talking," he eyed Jim with a stern expression, "I'm sure Jim here can wait until you're feeling better."

"I'm fine, but I really don't have much to say. I was heading over here, and looked down, and there she was. I knew she was deceased, but I checked her pulse on her neck and then her wrist just to be sure, and when I didn't get anything on either, I called the police. That was it."

"Must have been hard for you to go through that again," Max said.

I appreciated the reference to my husband. "It is what it is."

"Did you see anyone? Notice anything strange?" Jim asked.

"Nothing unusual, but like I told the police, I had things in my hands so I was paying attention to the pumpkins on the ground, which is probably how I noticed her in the first place. Have they figured out what happened to her?"

"You the one that smelled the almonds?" Jim asked.

I nodded.

"They think it was cyanide," Max said. "Sometimes it's got a faint smell of almonds, though not everyone can smell it. They've removed the pumpkins from the area and cleaned up. They're testing everything, and I'm assuming Traci, too."

I gasped. "Cyanide?"

The two men nodded.

"So they think someone poisoned her?"

Jim shrugged. "Don't know, but looks like they're fixin' to find out."

CHAPTER TWO

Hayden's voice went up several octaves. "Wait, what? Do you want me to come home?"
"Honey, I'm fine. I'm not going to fall apart because I found a woman dead in a pumpkin patch." I didn't explain to my daughter how the woman died. The last thing I needed was Hayden panicking more and then rushing home to take care of me.

She sighed heavily over the phone. "Mom, I worry about you."

"I know, but you can't come home every time something happens to me. You're not responsible for my care and well-being. I'm fully capable of taking care of myself."

"That doesn't stop the worrying."

"I know, and I appreciate it, but it's really annoying, so knock it off."

She laughed. "Yes, ma'am."

"Besides, you're a young woman with a life. Don't you have plans tonight?"

I put the phone on speaker and tossed a cup full of kibble

into a bowl for Allie and another one for Bandit, my most recent foster fail though I'd yet to fill out the paperwork.

"Is that dog food? I hear dog food, don't I? Is it for Bandit?"

"I plead the fifth."

"You got another dog?"

"Maybe."

"And you're replacing me yet again with a four-legged baby, aren't you?"

Allie barked just to drive the knife deeper into Hayden's heart.

"Allie, shush," I said. "You're upsetting the human."

"That's why you don't want me to come home. You don't want me to meet my newest arch nemesis."

"I don't want you to try and steal your newest arch nemesis."

She laughed. "What is she?"

"A pittie."

"Blue?"

"Yup. With a little white under her chin already."

"Oh, I'm already in love and I've never even met her."

"And you live in an apartment in Midtown. You can't have her."

"Mom, you have a hundred dogs already, you don't need another one."

"She followed me home. What was I supposed to do, tell her no?"

"You've told me no my entire life."

"That's different. You talk back."

"When can I meet her?"

"The festival is this weekend. She'll be there. She's trained, too." I set Allie's food bowl on the floor and told her to sit. She sat. When I released her for the food, she ate.

"I'll try to come, but I've got a deadline, so I'm not sure I can make it."

Later that evening, I researched cyanide poisoning online, and even though it was likely I was fine, I decided to go to the emergency room just in case. My research stated most people died within thirty minutes of poisoning, so the odds were that I was okay, but I wasn't clear on what the exposure issue was, having read that there is cyanide in things like chicken, something I eat often, so I decided I was better safe than sorry to get checked out.

When I explained who I was and what I'd been exposed to, the person at the emergency room desk had me in a room immediately. They drew blood and had me pee in a cup, something I always struggled to do upon request, but the doctor assured me that given the fact I was still alive, he was ninety-nine percent sure I was fine. The test would take twenty-four hours to be returned, and they wanted to admit me, but I declined. If I were to die, I didn't want it to be in the hospital, and I had things to do anyway. Dying wasn't on my to do list.

I left the hospital confident I was fine, and before I even got to my car, a detective from the police department called and asked if I could come in for a detailed interview first thing in the morning, just as I suspected would happen.

I arrived at the station at eight o'clock as planned. I'd never been in an interrogation room before, but it was exactly as I'd expected. Cold, emotionless, and full of stainless steel and metal with one of those big mirrored windows for others to check out the criminals without the criminals knowing they were there. I smiled into the window. I didn't think anyone was in there watching me, but maybe they were, so just in case, I showed them my pleasant side.

A stout man with broad shoulders and a balding head with an almost cone shape walked into the room. His short sleeve black polo shirt fit tightly over his muscled chest. "Mrs. Kingston?" He glanced at his papers as he read my name.

I adjusted my bottom in the uncomfortable seat. "Yes."

He thrust out his hand. "Detective Bruno. I'm the lead on the Fielding case. Thank you for coming." He pulled out the chair across from me and sat.

"Of course."

He skimmed through his papers and then looked up at me over the rim of his dark glasses. "I understand you're the one who found Ms. Fielding?"

"Yes, sir."

"Can you tell me about that?"

I detailed out what happened just as I had to Jim and Max and the officer the night before.

"How about the surroundings? Can you tell me if you heard anyone around you? Maybe what you saw on your way to the, what'd you call it, the pseudo pumpkin patch?"

I pondered on that, trying to step back in time to the moments I spent walking toward the patch. "I'm not really sure I remember much, but of course there were people around. Everyone's getting ready for the festival."

"Take your time." He tapped a pencil on the hard metal table. "Maybe you saw someone coming toward you, people off to the side?"

A picture of the scene developed in my head. "Come to think of it, I did see Jake talking to someone, but I don't think it was near the patch." The image became clearer, and I shook my head. "No, it wasn't. They were over by the Ferris wheel. He was talking to Jennifer Lee, one of the volunteers."

Detective Bruno took notes as I spoke. "Jake Fielding?"

"Yes, sir."

"Did you happen to hear what they were discussing?"

"No, I was too far away, but it kind of looked like they were arguing."

He glanced up from his notepad. "How so?"

She had her hands on her hips, and he was leaning back with his hands spread out in front of him. When my husband and I argued, which was rare really, I always had my hands on my hips."

He noted that and then lifted his head, making eye contact again. "Did you notice anything else in the area? Hear anyone talking? See Traci before you found her?"

"I did see her earlier, yes."

"And?"

"I saw her talking to Gina Palencia, another volunteer." I adjusted myself in the chair. "But that would be normal. They were working on the festival together. She was Traci's assistant."

He nodded.

"Oh." More came to me. "And I overheard a little of their conversation, too. Traci was upset because Gina booked a clown that looked like the one from the movie *IT* and she thought that was too much. Said it would upset the kids."

He smirked. "I can understand that."

"Me, too. Who thinks that's okay?"

He smirked again. "Clearly not you or Mrs. Fielding."

"Traci was pretty upset about it. Told Gina if she didn't cancel the clown, she'd remove her from the team. I can't believe I didn't think of this earlier."

"This kind of thing happens a lot, it's why we bring in witnesses. Once we start asking questions, they usually start remembering things they didn't realize."

"Oh, that makes sense."

He gave me a blank stare and then tapped the pencil on the table again. It must have been a nervous tick or something. "Anything else you can think of?"

I shook my head. "No, I don't think so."

He asked me a few more questions. Did I touch the body, about the smell, did I notice anything out of place, those kinds of things, and I answered honestly. When he walked me to the door, he shook my hand.

"Thank you for coming in. If we need anything else from you, we'll give you a call."

"Detective, do you have any idea who did this to Traci?"

"We have a list of suspects, yes, but that's all I can say at the moment. Though, I would expect an arrest to be made soon."

"I spoke to someone who said cyanide was found on the pumpkins near her. Is that what killed her?"

He released a long, slow breath. "You mentioned you smelled almonds, and the officer responding to the call knew cyanide can smell like them, so we are looking into it. The lab did test the pumpkins, and yes, there was evidence of cyanide on one of the pumpkins near the victim, but I can't confirm if that's the cause of her death. We have to wait for the autopsy results."

"When you have them, will you let the public know?"

"It's my understanding the public has already made an assumption, ma'am, but we will provide accurate information if the chief allows."

I nodded. "I was tested just in case."

"Given the effects of cyanide poisoning, if you had been affected, you'd likely be dead by now."

Detective Bruno wasn't the most sensitive guy on the block, but I didn't mind his bluntness. In fact, I appreciated it. "That's what the doctor said."

"I'd appreciate it if you'd keep our conversation private, ma'am. It will help with the investigation."

"Oh, absolutely."

He closed the door to the police station behind me.

I spent the rest of the morning working at the shelter. We'd received another seven dogs, but thankfully, four others had been adopted, so at least that was some good news. One of our pitties was pregnant, and we'd finally found a foster for her. I'd wanted to take her, but with the amount of dogs in and out of my house, and my time away, I wasn't sure I could be there enough for her. That was probably a good thing because when she had the pups, I would have likely ended up a foster fail for all of them.

I'd stopped back at the house before heading to the shelter, picked up Allie and my foster fail with the unsigned paperwork, Bandit. Bandit was a black lab I'd grown attached to, though I'd grown attached to every single dog I'd met, who was I kidding. When I received the extra life insurance policies I'd donated enough money to create an outside turf play area for the dogs, and the ones that played well had open play time when it wasn't blazing hot. The ones that didn't play well went out on their own until we worked with them enough to slowly merge them into the group. Allie and Bandit did fine with others, so bringing them allowed each to get some exercise and keep them used to being around other dogs.

Everyone talked about Traci Fielding and the possible cyanide poisoning, and until I assured them all I'd been two hundred percent cleared by the doctor, they'd kept their distance. Once they felt safe around me, they hounded in like

I knew something they didn't, and I almost wished I hadn't let them think I was safe to be around.

I liked to talk with people, but too much was never a good thing, and I didn't enjoy having my life put on a platter and served to people at their leisure. Call me cranky, Lord knows Hayden did most of the time, but since my husband's death, I'd kept to myself, and I'd adjusted to that just fine.

I spent extra time with two dogs, both pit bulls in need of extra love and attention. Dog fighting was alive and kicking, and we often received dogs that had been hurt and/or abused from a horrible life of fighting. While most people were afraid of them, I loved them extra because they needed it. They needed to develop trust and feel love, and it was my job to help them. The two I worked with, Lila and Stu, weren't aggressive, they were timid. But when their anxiety left, their wiggle butts nearly whacked their own big, boxy heads and practically knocked me over. It was glorious to see them come out of their shells, to roll onto their backs and let me rub their freckled bellies, massage their ears, and kiss their big square foreheads.

I had the best life. It just would have been better to share it with Sam.

One of the volunteers walked into the play area and shut the gate behind her. "Hey Missy, did you hear?"

I finished spraying off the turf. "Hear what?"

"They arrested Traci Fielding's husband thirty minutes ago."

I dropped the hose. "They what? Are you serious?"

"One of the volunteers, Alicia, is dating a cop, and he just texted her and told her."

I shut off the hose, picked it up, carried it to the holder, and wrapped it around it. "Gosh, I had no idea he was a suspect, or that they were even that close to arresting someone."

"Of course he was a suspect. The spouse is always the suspect. Don't you watch TV?"

I smiled. "Not enough to know that, I guess."

She eyed me up and down. "Well, I just thought you'd want to know."

I said thanks as she left the turf area.

Allie and Bandit lay on the turf and basked in the warm late afternoon sun. October weather was iffy in the Atlanta area, going from cool temperatures in the high fifties to low sixties in the mornings to mid-eighties in the late afternoons. Only a few times have we had a cold Halloween, and based on the weather patterns, I didn't think we'd have one this year.

"Come on pups, time to go inside."

The dogs inched their way off the turf, stretching as they did.

My cell phone rang and I pulled it from my back pocket.

"Hey Max, what's up?"

"Did you hear about Jake Fielding?"

"Just now, yes. I can't believe it."

"I'm shocked. I've known Jake for a long time, and I can't believe he'd do something like this. Doesn't make sense to me."

"I'm sorry. The police must have evidence to arrest him though, right?"

He breathed heavily. "One would think. Hey, can you grab a quick coffee? I'd like to talk to you again about what happened if you've got some time."

"Sure, but I already told you basically everything. I was planning to go grab lunch. I skipped breakfast this morning. Are you hungry?"

"I could eat. How about Atlanta Bread in thirty?"

"Make it twenty. I'm borderline hangry already."

"Then let's get some food into you before something bad happens."

I laughed and said I'd leave immediately.

I left Allie and Bandit, promising them I'd be back in a bit to get them, said goodbye to the rest of my babies, and headed over to Atlanta Bread.

He was already waiting at a table when I arrived, face down into his cell phone.

I tapped him on the shoulder when he didn't see me walk up. "You look like my daughter with that thing in your face like that."

He glanced up at me with his eyes wide. "Oh geez, I'm sorry. I didn't see you."

"Obviously. You can't see me with your face stuck in your phone."

He set the phone face down on the table. "Duly noted, ma'am."

I laughed. "You are too old to call me ma'am."

"It's a term of endearment."

"To whom, a grandmother?"

He smiled. Max had a nice smile. I had to give him that. He stood and offered me to walk in front of him. Atlanta Bread is an order at the counter deli style restaurant with sandwiches and soups. They have a great bread bowl with special fall soups, and I especially loved the pumpkin one. It's not always on the menu, but the owner adopted a dog from the shelter and sent me the October soup calendar a few weeks ago, so I knew it was available.

We ordered our food, got our drinks, and then sat at a corner booth.

"So, what's up?" I asked. Max and I were friends like I said, but he'd called for a reason, and I wanted to get to it.

"I'm worried about Jake. I don't think he did it."

"Why not?"

He blinked. "Why not?"

I nodded. "Sam always said he wasn't an ethical businessman, and we both know he's cheated on Traci multiple times. Committing murder could be the next step in that kind of life."

"Don't you think that's a reach?"

I shook my head. "Not really. Character traits are telling things, and they form patterns."

"So, you think he's guilty?"

"I didn't say that. I said it's plausible he progressed to killing. What makes you think he's innocent?"

He sighed. "I guess it's a theory of opposites for me. I know Jake's done some bad things in his life, everyone has, at least to some level, but I think he's got boundaries and limits, and murdering his wife? I just don't see that as a line he'd cross."

"What are you looking for from me?"

"I was hoping you could tell me what you said to the police."

"I've been asked to keep my comments private, Max. It's an investigation."

He grimaced. "Missy, I know, and I understand, but this is important. I really don't think he did it."

"Because of the opposites thing?"

"Because he told me, and I believe him."

"If he told you he didn't cheat on his wife, would you believe that, too?"

He leaned back in his seat and sighed. "Listen, I know Jake's not been a good husband, I'm not disagreeing with you on that. And yeah, I could use that whole, there's two sides to every coin but—"

"Three sides to the truth?"

He nodded. "Yes, that kind of thing, but I'm not going to do that. Jake cheated on Traci. More times than I probably know about, but he's under a lot of stress with the divorce and his businesses, and I just don't think he'd add more mistakes to the ones he's already made."

I wasn't sure what to do. Max pushed hard for me to believe in Jake's innocence, but I wasn't sure I was on board. I hadn't exactly said anything that would cause the police to arrest Jake, that much I knew, but my comment could have been the icing on the cake for sure. And if I told Max, and by some means, that information got out, I had no idea what would happen to the case. "Max, I…I'm not sure I can tell you anything. The detective was pretty insistent that I not share the information."

"Do you know Jennifer Lee?"

"Of course."

"Then you probably know Jake had a thing with her right?"

"I'd heard rumors."

"They weren't just rumors, they were true. But he broke it off recently, and Jen, she was really upset about it. She threatened him. Said she'd destroy him. Make him pay. Said if he could ruin her life, she could just as easily ruin his."

"Jennifer said that? That doesn't sound like her."

"I was there. I've never seen anything like it, and I would have said the same thing about her before, but not anymore. It was intense."

"So what're you saying?"

"I'm saying it's possible Jennifer could have had something to do with Traci's death."

I stiffened. "Have you told this to the police?"

He nodded. "And I'm assuming Jake has, too by now, but I'm worried something you said may have tipped the scale the wrong way."

I crossed my feet under the table and took a sip of soup. I was torn. Telling him would go against my promise to the police detective, but not telling him felt wrong, too, so I opted for the middle ground. I'd learned to do that during my marriage and child rearing years. "Max, if the police think there's a chance Jennifer had something to do with Traci's death, they'll look into it. That's their job."

"Not if they've already got their killer. They'll work on getting a conviction for him, and that's it. But if they have anything that could help turn the table…"

"I mean, I…I told the truth, and I'm comfortable with that, but that's all I can say about it."

He nodded. "But you saw him arguing with Jennifer yesterday, didn't you?"

Since he asked, he clearly already knew, and that annoyed me. "Why didn't you just ask me that in the first place? You're an attorney for God's sake Max."

"I'm sorry. Did you tell the police that?"

I nodded.

He breathed a sigh of relief. "Thank God."

"Are you going to represent him?"

"No. No. I handle real estate transactions. I'd get killed in a criminal trial."

"So what happens now?"

"He'll get a bail hearing, hopefully be released, and it'll go to trial."

"And you honestly believe he didn't kill Traci?"

"I'm sure he didn't."

"Because you think Jennifer Lee did."

He nodded. "Yes, Missy, I do, and I'm hoping you can help me find out."

I almost choked on my pumpkin soup. "Why would I help you find that out?"

"Because whoever killed Traci could have killed you, too. Whether the autopsy results are back yet or not, they will be in a matter of days, and we both know it's going to show cyanide poisoning, Missy. Had you touched that pumpkin, by, I don't know, tripping or whatever, you could be dead, too. Do you really want the wrong person going to prison?"

Max had a point, a very valid, important point. I could have died, and that would have left Hayden with zero parents. I at least owed it to her to make sure whomever killed Traci paid for it and wasn't left free to kill anyone else.

"So, what do you have in mind?"

"Since I'm a city council member, I can't do much in the public eye. I'm going to need you to get out and ask questions, find out what you can about Jennifer, maybe look into other people that didn't like Traci. All we need is reasonable doubt to keep Jake out of prison, but to get the killer, we'll need proof." He pressed his lips together, and his eyebrows furrowed, forming a long thin line up his forehead between them. "And honestly, I don't have a clue how to do that."

CHAPTER THREE

I'd spent a lot of time on my MacBook over the past few years, learning about dogs, dog training, grants, funding, and volunteering for shelters, as well as virtually everything else having to do with dogs, and I'd become sort of an expert. It didn't happen quickly, but in the process I learned about research and the best ways to go about it. I also spent a lot of time watching mysteries, the old fashioned kind like Agatha Christie, and less old fashioned, but still old to many, *Murder She Wrote*. I knew they were fiction, and I knew their means to solve murders were often impossible, or sprinkled with fairy dust and luck, but I also knew their cases were puzzles, and I liked puzzles, so I decided to think of Traci Fielding's murder as a puzzle.

And my first step to solving the puzzle was to figure out all the pieces. To do that I'd start with the obvious. Jake Fielding.

His bail hearing was the next morning, and though I wasn't sure I'd be able to see him, I headed over to the jail anyway. After going through two security systems, leaving my purse, cell phone, and belt in a small locker similar to the one I had in high school, I was allowed in a small meeting area to wait for him.

An officer escorted Jake in. I wasn't sure how I felt when I saw him. I was a bowl full of emotions mixed and blended into one large mass of uncertainty. I still wasn't sure he was innocent, but I wasn't exactly sure he was guilty either.

He sat in the chair across from me, a look of confusion and intrigue spread across his face. "I'm not sure to what I owe this honor, Mrs. Kingston."

I smiled. "I'm not sure exactly either, but we have a mutual friend, and he's been good to me since my husband died, so if for no other reason, I owe him a favor."

He smiled. "Max Hoover, I presume?"

Jake Fielding had an air of superiority and snobbery surrounding him. He always had. He lived in one of the wealthier communities in town and everyone knew he had a lot of money. It wasn't that he told people, it was just known, though I suspected the multiple businesses he owned were a big hint. But even so, he had the attitude to go along with the six thousand square foot home, indoor/outdoor pool, media room, and three expensive foreign cars. I wasn't jealous. We could have had all of that, too, but we never quite saw a reason. "Yes." I wet my lips, giving myself a moment to prepare my thoughts for what I wanted to say. "Max seems to think you're innocent."

"Max is correct."

I leaned back in my chair. "I'm not so sure."

"You don't like me much, do you Mrs. Kingston?"

"I have this weird thing about men that aren't faithful. I wouldn't call it dislike. Disgust seems to be a more appropriate word."

"Understood."

"But I do like Max, and he made a good point."

He raised an eyebrow. "And what was that exactly?"

"That if you didn't kill your wife, the person that did is still out there."

Jake looked me straight in the eyes. He didn't blink, he didn't flinch. "I can promise you I didn't kill my wife."

Sam was a serious and experienced businessman. He'd spent many years negotiating major contracts, and he'd learned to read people well. Over the years, he'd shared some of his techniques with me. One thing that stuck was how to tell when someone lied, and I'd used that successfully during Hayden's teenage years. Sam said to check her eyes. If they'd look down and to the right, she was lying. If she maintained eye contact, she wasn't.

Sam wasn't wrong about that kind of thing, and that's how I knew Jake Fielding didn't kill his wife.

"Then who do you think did?"

The chains attached to his feet rattled, and the table shifted up as he adjusted his legs underneath. "That's a hard question to answer."

"Max thinks one of your ex-lovers is the killer."

He furrowed his brow. "What? Who?"

I didn't have a whole lot of patience for Jake Fielding, and what little patience I did have was wearing thin fast. "Jake, come on, don't play games with me. There are plenty of other things I can do to repay Max's kindness." I realized to a man like Jake, that may have sounded a lot steamier than intended. In fact, it shouldn't have had any steam to it at all. I wasn't that kind of woman.

He breathed deeply. "I don't like to make presumptions."

"You're in jail for the murder of your wife. I don't think not making presumptions is an option at this point. If you know someone that could have, in any way, wanted your wife dead, you should tell someone. It doesn't have to be me, but tell someone."

He nodded. "You're right, Missy. I apologize. Of course,

you know from your conversation with Max about Miss Lee."

"Given your relationship with her, I think you can call her Jennifer."

He pressed his lips together. "Yes, well, Jennifer then. I saw you at the fairgrounds yesterday, and I'm assuming you saw our unfortunate miscommunication."

"Argument? Yes, I did. Care to tell me what that was about?"

He shrugged. "Let's just say Miss, er, Jennifer isn't happy with my decision to end our relationship."

Jake Fielding made my skin crawl so much I had to stop myself from flicking at the imaginary ants on my arms. "Jake, come on, cut the crap. If I'm going to do anything to help Max help you, then I need you to be open and honest." I held my arms out wide. "Or I'm out. And frankly, other than Max and your attorney, you don't have anyone on your side. The entire town knows about your multiple affairs and the public arguments with your wife. Oh!" I held up a finger, "And don't forget you selling the house and cars out from under her and then buying that new McMansion all for yourself. So either shape up or I'm shipping out."

Jake stared at me with his mouth slightly open. I stared back, my foot tapping lightly on the floor beneath the table. I was nervous. I didn't usually act so openly contentious, but I seriously did not like the man, and a woman was dead most likely because of his actions.

"You're right. I'm sorry."

It was my mouth that hung open that time. "You're what?"

He laughed a little. "Your husband always said you were a woman not to be messed with." He smiled and shrugged. "I'll be honest, I always thought he meant he wanted me to stay away from you."

"He probably did."

"Probably, but I think he also meant in regard to your strength. He said you were a force to be reckoned with."

I almost blushed, but then caught myself. "Sam was a good man."

"That he was. There are a few people I will tell my attorney to consider as having problems with my wife. Contrary to local rumors, and though I wasn't—am not—the best man, Traci wasn't always an angel."

Throwing your dead wife—the one you were accused of killing—under the bus was just low. I swallowed back that comment, though I was tempted to say it out loud. Very tempted. "Are you talking about additional former lovers?"

He shook his head. "There weren't as many as people think."

"Then who else would want Traci dead?"

"I think it's best I leave that information to my attorney until he says otherwise."

"That's fair. One more thing."

He raised an eyebrow.

"Where were you when Traci was killed?"

"I was at the fairgrounds. You know that."

"Yes, but at the time she was killed, specifically, where were you?"

"With Gina Palencia. She'd wanted to talk about the event. She had some concerns about Traci."

I didn't accomplish much in that meeting, though outside of getting a read on whether Jake was guilty or innocent, I wasn't exactly sure what I thought I'd accomplish. I didn't think he killed Traci, and because of that, I was more committed than ever to find out who did.

As I left the jail, another city council member, Rick

Morring, was going through the first section of security gates. When he saw me, he waved and asked me to wait inside the secured area. He cleared the check and smiled at me. "Missy Kingston, you're the last person I'd expect to see in jail."

I laughed. "Since I'm not behind bars, I don't think this counts, does it?"

"So, what brings you here? You finally decide to move forward with your pups and prisoners program?"

"Not yet. I don't have the manpower for it at the moment. One day though."

He nodded. "What you've done for the shelter, for those dogs, it's amazing. We're grateful for your service."

"Thanks, it's been as good for me as it has been for them, if not better."

He glanced toward the lockers where he needed to store his belongings before going into the meeting area of the jail.

"I won't keep you."

"No, no. It's okay. What brings you here today?"

"I came to see Jake Fielding."

His eyes widened. "Really? Interesting." He paused for a moment and then pointed his finger at me in that cheesy used car salesman kind of way. "You're the one that found his wife. I forgot about that."

I nodded. "I wanted to offer my condolences."

"To a murderer? How kind of you."

"Innocent until proven guilty, that's the way our justice system works, and since I know what it feels like to lose a spouse, I thought I should come by."

He winced. "Oh, well, yes, I'm sorry. I didn't mean to be heartless."

I plastered a smile on my face. "Of course not."

"Anyway, I best get inside. City council business and all." He tipped his head. "It was nice seeing you."

"You too."

I called Max on my way to the fairgrounds. "I stopped by the jail."

"And?"

"And Jake Fielding really is a pompous jerk, isn't he?"

He laughed. "Always has been, but that doesn't make him a killer."

"I think you're right about that."

"You don't think he killed Traci?"

I sighed. "No, I don't, but I still don't like him."

"I'm okay with that."

"He thinks Jennifer Lee should be a suspect."

"You already thought that might be the case."

I hadn't really given it enough thought to decide that was actually how I felt.

"And he really isn't a fan of Traci. Or wasn't, I guess."

"Marriage is hard. Divorce is harder. Trust me, I know from experience."

"I guess I was lucky."

"You were very lucky."

I changed the subject. I was okay for the most part, but sometimes the grief came back and overwhelmed me, and I didn't want it to happen then. "I'm on my way to the fairgrounds to check on the set up, and I don't know, maybe snoop around a little. Do you have any suggestions? Maybe someone I should talk to? Jake said he was going to let his attorney know who might have wanted Traci dead, but he didn't offer up any names to me."

"I don't know of anyone off hand, but let me see what I come up with. In the meantime, just listen. You'll hear something. We've had a murder, and it's the first one in town in over ten years. People are going to talk."

∼

Boy, was he right. People were talking, a lot. I wasn't immune to a good bit of gossip myself, so I understood. Those people that say they don't like gossip? I've never seen any of them walk away when someone's telling them some. I think everyone is at least a little interested in the latest and greatest, and when it's big, like a well known person's murder, it's bound to draw a lot of talk.

I happened to be the center of attention at the fairgrounds, and while that made my little amateur sleuthing deal easier, it was a bit overwhelming. I'd already been part of the gossip train when Sam passed, and I wasn't keen on jumping on that ride again.

I ran into Gina in the volunteer tent.

"Hey Missy. How are you?" She came toward me, her long brown ponytail whipping back and forth, and she sashayed my direction wearing a pair of four inch heels I would have tripped in after a few steps. "I've been so worried."

She hugged me, and I hugged her back, hiding my slight cringe in the collar of her pink sweater. I wasn't a touchy feely kind of person at all, unless it was family. "I'm fine, you don't need to be worried about me."

"Well, we all are. It's a tragedy, what happened to Traci, and you, you poor thing, you had to find her like that." She shook her head and made a *tsk* sound. "It's horrible. Just horrible. People are running around here like chickens with their heads cut off. No one knows what to do. It's like they've lost all sense of order because Traci's gone. Seriously, we have a festival to run. Someone has got to get it together."

"And that should be you, Gina. You're the assistant lead anyway. It's natural for you to step up and take charge."

She blushed. "You think? I wouldn't want to upset anyone."

"What would upset everyone is the festival tanking

because of what happened. I know I want it to be a success for Traci. In her honor. Don't you agree?"

She nodded. "Yes, yes. I do."

"Then you should say something to everyone." I glanced around the tent and took a quick head count. There were at least twenty volunteers there at the moment. "But first, can I ask you a question?"

"Of course."

"I heard you and Traci discussing the clown, and I…I was wondering if you ever resolved that."

She laughed and waved me off like it wasn't a big deal at all. "Of course we did. The clown's a go. She was fine about it after I explained my reasoning. It'll be fun. He's not going to scare people. He's more of a funny clown."

I nodded. "That's good."

"Anything else?"

I shook my head. "I was just curious."

"Missy, I adored Traci. Adored her. I mean, she had her things, you know? Things that drove people crazy of course, but she was a good egg, and I liked working with her." She glanced around the room. "Now, I think you're right. I think it's time for me to take charge and get this festival back in gear." She clapped her hands and then whistled. "Everyone gather around please. I have an announcement to make."

When everyone scooted toward the classically dressed woman in her big heels, she stood up on a wood picnic table. "Since Traci, God rest her soul, is gone, and I'm the assistant head volunteer, Missy Kingston here suggested I should take over and get the festival on track." She smiled at me, and from her glowing cheeks and slight wave of her hand, it felt like she was a celebrity appeasing her fans. "And that's exactly what I'm going to do." She blurted out a bunch of bru-hah-hah and go team go kind of speak, then proceeded to dole out a to do list a mile long, assigning tasks to everyone in the tent as well as people not there. She even gave herself an assistant and had her take notes. It was kind of impressive.

I headed over to the pooch party tent area to make sure everything was still in order. Though the fairgrounds had overnight security, I worried something would happen and kept a close watch on our space. Still good to go, I opted to take a walk around the festival itself and see what I could dig up.

People were talking about Traci's murder like it was the only news in town. I was surprised to hear most people felt Jake was guilty, and their opinions on his punishment were intense. Two women were especially angry and accusatory.

"He should get the chair."

"No, not the chair. That's too kind. He needs a public hanging."

I wasn't even sure if Georgia had the death penalty and I thought their comments were a bit extreme. "Why do you think he did it?" I asked the two women.

The one who opted for electrocution, a plus-sized blonde with the fashion sense of a super model—I envied that—said, "Because he did."

Well, there you go.

"Of course he did it," the other said. She didn't have the same fashion sense, and even though she dressed nicely, her attire suffered by comparison. "He wanted a divorce, and Traci was fighting him tooth and nail."

"As she should," the blonde said. "She was there when he got his start. If not for her, he wouldn't be the man he is today."

"A man in jail accused of killing his wife?" I asked. From their slack jaws, it might not have been the right question.

"You don't understand. You don't know what it's like. You

have a good—" Blondie stopped herself before sticking her knee-high boot into her mouth.

The other woman, whose name I couldn't for the life of me remember, glanced around the fairgrounds like she was looking for someone. Anyone but me.

"No marriage is perfect. They all have their ups and downs." I smiled confidently, pushing my shoulders back a bit. "But a marriage doesn't have to be bad to have issues. Everyone has skeletons in their closet. It's quite possible Jake's innocent and someone else killed Traci."

"She's right, you know. Traci wasn't easy to work with, Shelly. You know that."

Kim! That was her name. "I've heard that a few times, Kim, and though I haven't worked with her much, I think I can see how some felt that way. She was very specific in her requests and what she wanted."

"She was a shrew," Kim said.

Goodness, I wouldn't have gone that far. Cruelty was alive and well at the fairgrounds. "Shrew's are people too," I said.

I wasn't making a joke, but they both laughed.

"What if Jake didn't do it?" I pointed to Shelly. "You just said she wasn't all that easy to work with." I then pointed to Kim. "You called her a shrew. Isn't it possible someone else thought the same, or thought poorly enough of her to want her dead?"

They both stared at me.

"Well, I guess it's possible," Kim said.

"Maybe. You never really know people anymore," Shelly said.

I didn't want to be a part of gossip, but my interviewing skills were limited to foster and shelter volunteers. Murder investigations weren't my area of expertise. "So, Jake could be innocent, and that means the killer is still out there."

Shelly gasped. "Oh, that would be awful. What if they weren't trying to kill Traci, but wanted to stop the festival?"

Kim's eyes popped open and she jumped up onto her tiptoes. "I heard they did something to the pumpkins. What if they weren't trying to kill Traci, and instead wanted to kill festival attendees?"

I'd just opened a can of worms I probably should have kept shut and tucked far away in the bomb shelter Sam built in our basement. "I don't think someone was trying to cause any mass murder by pumpkin. The festival isn't until Friday. Planning ahead is one thing, but that's a little much."

Shelly giggled. "You're probably right. And come to think of it, I did see Traci and that no good tramp that slept with her husband arguing earlier. I wouldn't put it past her if she wanted to take Traci out."

I raised my eyebrow. "No good tramp?"

Kim smirked. "Jennifer Lee. I saw it, too. She was all up in Traci's face talking about how Traci needed to get over it already. I think Jennifer wanted her happily ever after, but we all know that won't happen with a cheater like Jake Fielding. Poor tramp's ending up a happily never after." She laughed. "That last part was my words, not hers."

"You heard them arguing?"

"Uh huh. I wasn't even ten feet away from them," she said.

Shelly agreed. "I was on the other side, but I heard them, too."

"Have you gone to the police with that?"

Shelly blanched. "Oh, gosh, no. Why would I do that? I don't want to get involved."

I pressed my heels into the ground. "Oh-kay. Well, I think you should. Anyone that was seen arguing with Traci on the day of her murder is a potential suspect. Didn't the police interview you yesterday?"

"Not me. I left before she was killed," Shelly said.

"I did, too. I had to pick up Charlie from day care."

"So, when did you see them arguing?"

Shelly shrugged. "Maybe an hour or so before I left, which, from what I gather was around the time this whole mess started."

"You really should tell the police."

"Do you think we should tell them about Rick Morring then, too?" she asked.

"What about Rick?"

Kim sucked in a breath and shook her head. "You mean you don't know?"

My jaw clenched. The two women must have thought I was a rabbit and they were dangling carrot scraps near my face. Did they think it was funny? Just in case, I had no intention of giving them any satisfaction. "Listen ladies, I have a lot of work to do for the festival. If you know something, you should go to the police. It's the right thing to do."

As I pivoted around on my heels to leave, Shelly grabbed my arm. "Rick Morring wants your part of the festival shut down. He was all up in Traci's face about it, too."

"She's right." Kim nodded as she spoke, as if that would make her statement more important. "I saw it myself. Said he'd make sure you couldn't be here next year if he had to get a new festival organizer. Traci was not happy."

"Nope, not happy," Shelly said.

"What? Why? Why would he say those things?"

They both shrugged. Shelly added, "I've heard he thinks the dogs are a danger to people, and you having them out like that can put a huge financial burden on the city. I'm not saying that I agree with him, I'm just repeating what I heard."

Kim raised her hand. "Me, too. I heard it, too."

I inhaled deeply and swallowed back what I wanted to say as I watched a group of people a few feet away scatter in various directions, one being Rick Morring. "That's good to know, but I still think you should go to the police." I couldn't say that enough. I smiled at both of them. "Have a great day, ladies."

They smiled, and I made a beeline straight for Rick Morring.

CHAPTER FOUR

"Rick, wait up." I jogged to catch up with him as he flipped around toward me.

It was just a flash, but I could have sworn he'd grimaced when he saw it was me. "Oh, Missy Kingston, we're running into each other a lot lately."

"Seems that way, doesn't it?" I caught my breath. "Listen, I heard you have some concerns about the dogs at the festival. If you have a moment, I'd like to discuss it with you."

He balled his hands into tightly clenched fists and then released them. "Concerns? I'm not sure what you're talking about." He sped up his pace, and I kept up with him.

"The concerns you shared with Traci Fielding. Something along the lines of you wanting to keep the dogs out of public places because it wasn't safe for the citizens of town." I thought I'd dialed back my attitude, but it was pretty darn clear in my tone.

No one messes with my pups.

His neck stiffened and the cords on each side swelled like hoses filling with water. "As I said, I don't know what you're talking about." He glanced at his watch. "And really, I've got a lot to do today, so I'm not sure I have time to discuss this." He flipped back around and headed the direction he was going before I caught up with him.

"Have you told the police you were arguing with Traci Fielding shortly before her death?"

He froze, and then a few seconds later, he turned around and smiled, but not a happy smile, a forced, obligatory, I-don't-like-you-but-I'm-doing-my-best-to-fake-it kind of smile. "Mrs. Kingston, I was at the police station for a city council issue, and whomever told you I was having an argument with Traci Fielding is misinformed. We were discussing matters regarding the festival. She wasn't thrilled with something I said, but it was in no way an argument, and I certainly did not kill the woman."

"Matters like my pooch party."

A sheen of sweat developed on his balding forehead. "Mrs. Kingston—"

I held up my hand to stop him from going further. "Every dog brought to any of my pooch parties is a well-trained, well-behaved dog that responds well in social environments, Mr. Morring. Those dogs are constantly exposed to people, volunteers who work with them on a daily basis, and to children who come and help at the shelter. If any of my dogs, and none to date so far, show any aggression toward humans, we don't bring them. We don't keep them at the shelter either. And as a member of our city council, you should know that. Those dogs, upon evaluation, are sent to a sanctuary farm about forty-five minutes north of here where they are supported by a grant to feed and care for them until it's their time to cross the bridge. Our community isn't in danger. Though," I thrust my hip to the left and planted my hand on it. "Many of our dogs can tell a bad person when they smell him. I invite you to come to the pooch party this weekend and check that out. See how it works for you, that kind of thing."

His lip curled and he shook his head as he turned again to leave.

"Oh, and one more thing. I guess you're getting that replacement you threatened Traci with now after all."

He pivoted slowly back toward me and stared directly into my eyes. "Have a nice day, Mrs. Kingston."

I flung my hand up and gave him a little wave. "You too, Councilman."

As he walked away, I stood there fuming, doing my best to calm my nerves and keep my head from spinning around in circles and flying off, though admittedly, that would have been the perfect event for a Halloween Festival.

Gina Palencia ran up to me as I walked toward the pooch party area. "Missy, thank God you're here. I'm so sorry this happened. Who let you know? I was just getting ready to call you."

My heart picked up its pace. "I was just coming to check on the—what's going on? Was someone else killed?"

Her mouth dropped, and she waved her hand as if to dismiss the possibility. "No, no. Of course not. It's your area. It's been vandalized. It's a wreck. We've already called the police. They're on their way."

My mood flipped from cranky to panicked in seconds. "My area? It's what?" I took off at a slow sprint toward the pooch party area, and when I saw it, my blood boiled.

"How did this happen?" I stepped into the middle of the turfed area and stared at the pumpkins smashed all over the place.

"Ma'am, you need to step out of here immediately, and please have one of our team remove your shoes. We don't want you touching them."

"But I'm the—" I glanced at my boots which had the

insides of pumpkin covering my toes. "Oh, no. You don't think?" The feint smell of almonds lingered in the air.

The officer guided me from the pooch park over to the makeshift desks. "So, you run this part of the festival?"

I nodded. "I work with the dogs. What's going on? Do you think there's cyanide on the pumpkins? I can smell almonds."

"We can't be sure, ma'am, but we aren't taking any chances."

Another member of the police department, a woman dressed in a white, short sleeve polo shirt and khaki pants with gloves on came over and removed my boots and socks. I'd just bought the things a week before, and they weren't cheap.

"Wait," I said before she took them away. "Can you tell me if you smell almonds on them? I can in the air, but I'm not sure I stepped in anything."

"How 'bout we keep that decision to the professionals?"

"So what, I'm just supposed to walk around barefoot? In October, at a fairgrounds?" I realized the absurdity of my question, but I didn't care. Walking barefoot on an often used blacktop area came with its own set of problems.

"Potentially die or walk cautiously to your car? Doesn't sound like a choice to me."

And bam, she put me right in my place, a place where there really are stupid questions. "I understand."

The officer smiled at me. "And we'll need to get photos of them for prints, too."

If they'd want to compare those to prints outside of the turfed area, they'd be doing that for months.

Max stepped up from behind me. "Missy, are you okay?"

I turned around and smiled at Max, and then when I caught a glimpse of Rick Morring next to him, I let out a sigh. "Yes, I'm fine Max, thanks for asking."

"Did you see who did this?"

I shook my head. "I just got here, and I walked right into the splattered pumpkins." I glanced at my bare feet. "And now I'm shoeless."

Rick chuckled. "Could be worse."

Max glared at him. "Bad timing, Rick."

He blushed. "Oh, I didn't mean it like that."

I narrowed my eyes at the man. "Of course you didn't."

Max's held swiveled between Rick and I. "Uh, so, do they know anything then?"

I shrugged. "Not that I know of, but since that woman over there in the white shirt stripped my feet, I suspect they're worried about cyanide poisoning again."

Rick raised an eyebrow. "Really?" He stared at my feet and then back at the scene playing out on the turf. "I can't imagine why anyone would want to harm the dogs. We all love having them here."

I wanted to kick him in the shin. "They're not harming the dogs. That's someone making a statement."

"What kind of statement?" Max asked.

"Maybe they're saying they don't want the dogs here." I made eye contact with Rick while I spoke. "And they think if they threaten me like this, I'll pull out of the festival."

"Who would do that kind of thing?" Max asked.

I glanced at him. "I don't know. Rick, who do you think doesn't want the dogs here?"

I caught the look of anger in his eyes, but it quickly disappeared. "I don't have a clue, but I'm sorry, I've got an appointment I have to get to." He smiled at Max. "Max." When he looked at me, his eyes became little slits of dark brown and white. "Missy."

As he walked away, I clenched my fists and pressed them into the sides of my thighs. "I do not like that man."

Max laughed. "Morring? Why not?"

"Because he's a bold faced liar, that's why." I sat on the

table in the covered area of the pooch party tent. "Did you know he was arguing with Traci Fielding about getting rid of the pooch party here? He told her he wanted me gone because the dogs aren't safe for the community, all shortly before I found her."

He opened his mouth and pushed his tongue slightly forward. When he spoke, I saw the disbelief all over his face. "What? No way. Rick's always said he loves the shelter programs. Whoever told you that is wrong."

"No, they're not, and no, he doesn't. He made it clear to me just a few minutes before I came here." I narrowed my eyes and squinted at the turf area. "What if he did this to scare me? What if there is cyanide on the smashed pumpkins? I smelled almonds, by the way. What if he was trying to kill the dogs?" I propelled myself off the table and winced when my bare feet hit the hard, rocky blacktop. I cautiously walked over to the police on the scene as Max walked next to me.

"Missy, no. You're not going to say something to the police, are you? This is Rick Morring we're talking about. A city council member."

I stopped and tried to remain grounded emotionally. "Of course I'm going to say something. I have to. The detective told me to tell him anything I knew. He didn't say to leave things out that happened after our interview."

I picked up my speed, tiny rocks be darned. "Excuse me, miss?" I tapped on the back of the police officer in front of me. "Is Detective Bruno coming?"

She flipped around and smiled when she saw my feet. "We've got your boots, don't we? Nice ones. They look new."

"Thank you, and yes, they are. I'm hoping I'll get them back. About Detective Bruno…" I didn't have to say anything else because the detective appeared a few feet away.

I called out to him, he glanced over at me, smiled, and headed my direction.

"Missy, come on," Max said. "I know I wanted you to help me with Jake, but you can't think—"

"Max, do the math. A woman was seen arguing with him about my dogs, and that woman's dead. Suddenly smashed pumpkin appears in the pooch party turf, just after Rick tells me he wants to eliminate the parties in public entirely. How can you see it differently?"

He exhaled. "You're right. I can't."

I explained my theory to Detective Bruno.

He nodded and took down notes.

"And I saw him at the station when I went to the jail," I said, my voice stern and determined. "I'm not sure you've got the right guy behind bars, detective."

He smiled at me, and a slight chuckled escaped his lips. "Ma'am, how about you let us do the police work?"

My patience hung by a hair. "Detective, you should at least look into it." I held up my foot. "I walked into that turf with the smashed pumpkins and smelled almonds. What if there's cyanide on them? Then you definitely don't have the right guy for Traci's death. Am I wrong?"

He eyed my feet, and I blushed because I was in desperate need of a pedicure. "Ma'am, we're testing the pumpkins, but I think you need to get back to the hospital and have yourself tested just in case."

I hadn't thought about that.

"Marx," the detective hollered to an officer. "Get some plastic booties here for Ms. Kingston and get her to the ER."

"I can—"

"I'll go with you," Max said.

The officer got us to the emergency room in ten minutes, and in traffic to boot. I would have been impressed if my stomach wasn't all in knots from him weaving in and out of traffic at a speed that had to be ten miles above the speed of light.

I undressed and changed into a cheap hospital gown with strings that tied in the back. I asked the nurse for a second one, so I could put it on backwards and tie it in the front. With Max there, I didn't want any peep shows happening by accident. Not that he'd see me in it anyway, but just in case.

Everyone that entered the room like before had masks on and special gloves and stayed as briefly as possible. An hour later I had to give Max the key to my house where he picked up a pair of clean jeans, socks, and another pair of boots to bring back for me.

A tall, skinny, and bald doctor that had a face full of Shar Pei wrinkles came into my room. "Mrs. Kingston, I'm Doctor McAllister. We have your test results back."

"I thought they took twenty-four hours?"

"If you'd gone to a doctor's office yes, but here, our lab is pretty fast."

"Am I going to be okay?" I assumed I would be given the fact that I'd been there for over two hours already and was still alive.

He smiled. "We found a small amount of cyanide on your jeans, but further testing of your feet shows no signs."

"So, there was cyanide in the pumpkin, and it got on my pants?"

"I can't say where the cyanide came from, but we're sending the pants over to the police department anyway."

"But I'm okay?"

"Yes, ma'am. If you had any touch your feet, which miraculously doesn't appear to be the case, it was miniscule." He jotted something on a piece of paper and handed it to me. "Follow these directions, and if you see any signs I've listed, you need to get back to us immediately. In the meantime, my staff will prepare a cyanide antidote kit just in case. Give us a few minutes and we'll be back."

"Is this something that will hurt?"

"No, I'm confident it won't bother you a bit."

A short time later, Max brought back my clothing and drove me back to the fairgrounds to get my car.

"How many dogs do you have now? I counted two at your place." He shot me a quick smile as we headed to the fairgrounds.

"That's all I have now. You didn't happen to let them out, did you?"

"I did. They both ran to the door and jumped on it, so I figured they needed to take care of business."

I smiled. "Those are the horrible dogs that are a threat to the community."

He frowned. "I'm sorry."

"For what? The fact that I could have died, or the fact that someone, very likely your friend and council member, is the one that tried to kill me."

"Yes."

I shifted my eyes from the road to him. "You're forgiven."

"They're releasing Jake Fielding."

"They should arrest Rick Morring. I think he did it."

"I'm not sure they have a suspect now that Fielding's in the clear."

"They need to catch this killer quickly. We have a festival in a few days."

"Agree, but it's not that simple. They need solid evidence and there just isn't any at the moment. At least not that I'm aware of."

That was ludicrous, and Max knew it. "What else do they need? Another victim?" I leaned my head back on the head rest. "I can't believe this is happening. All I wanted to do was help these poor dogs find homes, and the festival was the perfect place to do this. If Traci's death is somehow related to the pooch parties, I'll never forgive myself, especially if it's Rick Morring that killed her."

"They'll do a thorough investigation, and if they find evidence to charge Rick, they will. You know that."

"I don't know what other kind of evidence they need. He's attached to all of it."

He pulled into my driveway, shut off his car, and twisted his body to face me. "Missy, you have to look at this from an investigative angle."

"Like you? You yourself said you're not the right kind of attorney for this, so how would you know anything about investigating or evidence?"

"I did take some classes on this during law school. And besides, I've been a part of this city for years. You know that. I've worked closely with the police on all sorts of cases because that's what city council members do, and this case will be investigated, and they will find out who killed Traci and who tried to hurt you."

"Not me, my dogs." I sucked in a breath. "The turf. I'm going to have to replace the turf. The dogs can't go on it. There could be cyanide in the crevices of the fake grass." I pulled my phone from my purse and swiped through my contacts looking for the turf company I'd used before.

"Wait. I mean, yes, definitely order more turf. I'm sure the police have taken it by now anyway. But before you throw Rick under the bus, I think you need to dig deeper. Find out more. Rick's not a bad guy."

I rolled my eyes. "That's exactly what you said about Jake Fielding. Is there anyone you don't like in this town?"

He smiled. "One or two people, but I don't think either one of them is the killer either."

"Is there anyone you do think is? Someone that's a bigger jerk than Rick Morring maybe?"

"Okay, he's kind of a jerk at times, yes, but I don't think he'd do anything illegal to stop your program."

I stepped out of the car. "I appreciate your input, but I don't want to put my animals at risk because of some jerk that is scared of dogs."

He'd already jumped out of his car and jogged to me. "I think you're wrong about whoever did this wanting to hurt your dogs and not you. What if it's both? What if someone else had a similar conversation with Traci Fielding, killed her, and then decided to just be done with the problem entirely and kill you, too?"

I stopped at my front door and turned around, ignoring the dogs barking in the window. "You think someone else could have done this, and I'm the target?"

"I don't know, but I think we need to find out."

And after coming up with a quick plan, that's what I decided to do.

CHAPTER FIVE

The plan wasn't all that great, but it was a start, and Sam always said it was better to start with a plan, even if it changed right away.

Oh, how I wished my husband was with me still. What would he think? How would he handle it? Would he fight to have Rick Morring arrested? Would he even agree he was the killer? Probably not. Sam had a sense about things, about people. That's what made him a good businessman. I missed having him to bounce things off of.

After several minutes of me sitting in the chair with two large and heavy dogs standing on my lap giving my face an icky dog breath washing, which I laughed my way through—with my mouth closed, just in case—I fed the pups and took them for a walk around the property. Sam and I had five acres of land, and I'd always said when we retired to a home in the mountains, I wanted enough land for a dog sanctuary. I'd tried to convince him to let me start one at our current house, but he said five acres wouldn't be enough space for every dog this side of the Mason Dixon line, and he knew I'd go after them all.

Sam knew me well, better than I knew myself most times.

As we walked, Allie rolled in God only knew what while Bandit jumped and ran and barked at worms. Bandit was afraid of worms, and I understood. Their slimy wiggliness made me uncomfortable, too.

We sat in the gazebo in the middle of the property and stared out at our homemade doggie park, what I'd grown to call our land. I'd brought them a thermos of water and poured it into bowls I'd stored in a small trunk in the gazebo. They took a few sips and dropped to the ground panting to cool off.

I stood and leaned against the railing on the backside of the gazebo, running my hand along the white painted wood, watching the water ripple in the small pond we'd added a few months before Sam died. We'd created the space for a few reasons. We wanted a quiet place on our property where we could sit and relax, forget about the stresses of the day, and just enjoy each other's company, but we also designed it as a place for Hayden to one day get married. She'd always said she wanted to be married at home, and she loved the idea of an outside wedding. Sam was thrilled to build the gazebo with our help, and I was glad that where she'd planned to marry someday would have a piece of her father there for her, too.

Allie stretched and slowly pushed her way up to stand next to me. I smiled and rubbed her ears. Why would anyone be afraid of such a loving soul? Pit bulls were originally used as nannies for children in Europe. They were kind and gentle animals by nature, but like humans, could be raised wrong, and that impacted who they became.

If I could adopt every one of them, I would.

Bandit, on the other hand, was a big mush ball of drool and hair, and though he was smart in many ways, he'd lacked dog sense, as I liked to call it. Bandit thought every living being was his friend—except worms—and wanted nothing more than to love on them all. He did not understand that his eighty-pound bundle of love intimidated other animals. He also thought he was a lap dog, and even though he was a lab, a breed that loved water, he couldn't swim. And he snored. Loudly.

He made me laugh on a daily basis, and I was thrilled to call myself a complete foster failure.

Bandit dragged himself from the ground and came over to see what Allie thought was so great over by me. He nudged my leg with his snout and rubbed the side of his muzzle against me, his way of saying hello.

"You two ready to head back? I've got to figure out who's trying to stop us from adopting out your buddies."

They wagged their tails and took off galloping through the grass. They got back to the house faster than me, though in my defense, I only had two legs to their four, and I was several years older. We headed in through the back and they immediately emptied the water bowl. As I filled it, my Ring doorbell chimed on my phone. I checked the video and saw Gina Palencia standing there with a plastic food container in her hands and groaned. Surprise visits weren't something I enjoyed.

I answered the door via my phone. "Hey Gina, I'll be right there." I switched off the video and headed to the front door. I smiled. "Modern technology. Sam installed it before he—" I stopped myself. Everyone knew Sam was dead, and I knew it made people uncomfortable when I brought it up.

"Oh, Missy, I was so worried about you. I heard about the cyanide on the pumpkins, and I watched the police take away the turf. Whatever will you do?"

The turf. Darn it, I totally forgot to order more. I'd do that as soon as she left. I just hoped that would give them enough time to deliver it. The roll wasn't too big, but it was large enough that I'd had to have people tie it on the top of my car to get it anywhere.

I opened the door further. "Would you like to come in?"

She hesitated when she saw Allie and Bandit, who were both standing behind me. Allie's ears were down, and Bandit, God bless him, wagged his tail because he'd never once met a stranger.

I smiled at her. "Don't worry about them." I escorted her in as I scooted the dogs to the large keeping room attached to the kitchen. I'd added a portable kids fence there for times like this, when someone appeared uncomfortable with my dogs, or when one of the fosters needed a warm up time around strangers, or I just needed to get something done without a snout where it didn't belong. Bandit knew the drill, but Allie was a little put off by having to be fenced in. Her slightly slanted eyes widened, and she barked her disapproval.

"I know, baby but give me a few minutes with Gina. You'll be fine."

Gina tilted her head and pointed toward the dogs. "Do you think he understands you?"

"I'm pretty sure *she* does. It might just be the tone or volume of my voice, but I think she understands the meaning if not the actual words."

"Wouldn't that be great if that worked with humans, too?"

I laughed. "A miracle, for sure."

She set the plastic food container on the counter. "I wanted to bring you something. You've been through a lot recently, and I thought you might not want to deal with making yourself a homecooked meal." Her eyes studied my kitchen. "It must be hard cooking for one after so long."

I nodded. "It was an adjustment, but it's not as hard as people think."

"Oh, well." She waved her hand and shook her head at the

same time. "I shouldn't have said that. I don't want you to feel uncomfortable."

"It's okay."

"It's taco soup. Really, it's a spicy Mexican flavored chili, because of its thickness, but the recipe is called taco soup."

I opened the container and the heavy spicy aroma flowed out. Cumin, one of my favorite spices, burst from the dish and enveloped my nose, and I was immediately hungry, but already had a plan for my dinner. "It smells wonderful, Gina, thank you." I placed the container in the freezer.

She smiled. "So, they've released Jake Fielding."

"Yes, I've heard."

"I guess since they found cyanide on the fake grass, they decided he couldn't have killed his wife."

"Did they make it public that they found cyanide?" I assumed they would since it was on my jeans, but I hadn't heard anything official.

"It's not public, but you know how these things go. Everyone knows already. Good for Jake though, isn't it?"

I shrugged. "He could have paid someone to do his dirty work. Who knows?"

"Do you think that?"

I filled my coffee pot with water from my refrigerator. "Would you like a coffee? I have decaf since it's after five o'clock."

"Yes, that would be lovely. Thank you."

I made a full pot, placed two cups with saucers and spoons and cream and sugar on the counter. "Have a seat."

She pulled a barstool out and sat.

"I'm not sure who killed Traci," I said as I poured coffee into the two cups. I've been considering possibilities, and there are a few."

"You're considering possibilities? Why is that?"

I stirred the cream in my coffee. "Because they made it personal when they tried to harm my dogs."

She added a spoonful of sugar to her coffee, but no cream. "Do you really think Rick Morring is responsible?"

Her comment, bold as it was, came out of left field. "What makes you say that?"

"There's been talk. I guess someone saw the two of you discussing something about the pooch parties, and neither of you looked happy, so you know how it goes. It just spun into that from there I guess."

"That's kind of a stretch, don't you think?"

She set her coffee cup down. "Oh, I don't know. I just meant—" She exhaled. "Well, as the new head of the festival, several of the volunteers have come to me, you know, with their thoughts, ideas, suggestions, that kind of thing."

She'd been the festival head for all of a day, but I guess I could see that happening. "And they're talking about Rick Morring and I having a private discussion?"

"Nothing's private in festival planning, Missy."

I half-laughed, but only because it was obnoxiously true. "And what are they saying?"

"That Morring made it clear to Traci he wanted your part of the festival removed, and he said as much to you."

I swallowed a large gulp of coffee. "Has he said anything to you?"

She stiffened. "Well, he mentioned it the other day, but not since I've been in charge."

"And what exactly did he say?"

She glanced at my pups lying on fluffy dog beds on the floor and chewing on Benebones. "Just that he thought it was dangerous for the community."

I exhaled as I smiled over at my babies. "Do those two look dangerous to you? Did they threaten you in any way when I let you in?"

She hesitated but smiled. "Oh, no. Of course not. They're darling, really."

"I've worked hard with the shelter dogs, had many of them successfully trained and adopted out. I'm even working on a training program with the inmates at the county jail which will benefit the dogs and the people. We've been to dozens of events, and not one dog has harmed anyone. Unless you count possibly being kissed to death, my dogs aren't threatening at all." I felt the blood boiling in my veins, and a wave of red heat rose up my neck. "It's unbelievable to think people believe I would risk their safety."

"I agree. That's why I'm wondering if you think Rick is a potential suspect. He did make it obvious he wanted the dogs gone, and Traci wanted nothing to do with that."

"Well, I appreciate Traci's devotion." And I wished I could tell her that, too.

"Who do you think did it, Missy?"

"I'm not sure, but what I think doesn't matter. The police will investigate, and they'll find out."

"But you want to know, don't you? Isn't that why you went to the jail to talk to Jake?"

My eyes widened. "Is anything in this town private?"

She leaned back on the barstool and laughed. "Are you kidding? You know the saying, two can keep a secret if one of them is dead."

I played hide and seek with the dogs, something that every dog I've had loved. It helped work on their training skills for stay and come, and it kept their minds busy, which always wears dogs out. And, it was fun for me, too.

I commanded them to sit and stay in the keeping room

and then I tiptoed to the office at the front of the house and hid underneath Sam's desk. Bandit would likely know where to look and Allie would follow suit, but only because Bandit and I had played the game before and Allie was new to the program.

"Come find me," I whispered. Humans probably wouldn't have heard that, but the dogs took off running, their nails tapping on the wood floors as they rushed toward the office. Allie ran right past me, not even bothering to give me a glance, but Bandit bent down on her front legs and wiggled the back half of her body like she'd discovered a long-lost toy. I crawled out of the cramped space and patted them both on the head.

"Good babies." I handed them each a small treat. "Okay, you ready to go again?"

I put them in places on opposite sides of the office, where of course I had dog beds. I had dog beds in every room of the house leaving out the guest bedrooms because in there, they didn't need them. All the dogs thought the empty guest beds were theirs.

They both stayed, their little tails sweeping on the beds with excitement and anticipation as I tiptoed again out of the room, down the hall and into the pantry of the kitchen. I left the door cracked open.

"Come find me," I whispered again, and they took off once more.

They searched the keeping room, the bathroom, and the formal dining room, finally coming back to the kitchen. Before they checked the pantry, they did a quick sweep of the cooking area and then Allie, bless her heart, caught a glimpse of the pantry door open and made a beeline for it. Probably because she knew the treats were in there, though I couldn't be sure.

She popped the door open further with her snout and peeked behind it.

"Good girl," I said, cheering her on for her win.

Bandit came in and wiggled his back half again with joy.

"Aw, you two are the best puppies!" I handed them both another treat, which they took to separate parts of the house and ate.

I dropped onto the couch and flipped on the TV. "Okay, mommy needs a little break. I'm not as young and vibrant as you two."

I searched through the channels and clicked on something that looked interesting, a remodel show on HGTV, but I didn't really pay attention. Instead, I thought about what had transpired over the past day.

It struck me as odd that Gina knew the things she knew. I understood that people gossiped, and I realized word traveled swiftly, but it all seemed off. Had she approached people for their thoughts or to find out what they knew? What was Gina up to? Her actions didn't feel like curiosity to me. They felt like they had purpose attached to them, though I wasn't quite sure what that purpose could be.

I shuffled to the kitchen and opened the freezer. I pulled out the chili and set it on the counter even though I'd already had tuna salad prepared for my meal. I grabbed a bowl from the cabinet and as I went to scoop some of the wonderful smelling mix into it, I stopped.

Both dogs sauntered over, and Bandit drooled on my left while Allie's nose twitched on my right. I eyed the taco soup and groaned. I took the container and scooped it out, but into the sink instead. I turned on the water and stuffed it all into the disposal and then flipped the switch to turn it on. The chili went down the drain.

"Sorry babies, this might smell delicious, but I promise you, your tummies won't be happy." I wanted the spicy smelling treat too, but something stopped me from having it. That something was the fear that it might be laced with cyanide. I gave them another dog treat, though we all knew that wasn't the smell they wanted, and made myself a tuna salad sandwich.

The next morning, I followed my morning routine. My routine was different than when Sam was alive. Everything was different than when Sam was alive, and though I knew that logically, it didn't always matter. I wasn't much of an early breakfast eater, but I'd created a routine to provide myself stability. The thing about grief was that it never ended. It lessened, and was less frequent, but it still came, and often when we least expected it. That simple small routine change had almost broken me, but I'd accepted it, discovered my new normal, and found ways to keep my life full, though they never quite filled the hole in my heart.

I scooped enough kibble into the dog's bowls to feed a small horse and laughed at that because weight combined, Bandit and Allie were not at all light. They were the size of a small horse, and they ate like one, too.

Max called while I was in the shower, so I finished getting ready, got the dogs into the car, and returned his call on my way to the shelter. I had to work with a few of the trainers and dogs at nine o'clock but wanted to say hello to the rest of my dog crew beforehand.

"Hey, I saw that you called. What's up?"

"Jake's out, and it looks like the police are working on a few other leads."

"That's great. I had an interesting conversation with Gina Palencia last night. She said people have been talking and—"

He interrupted me. "Missy, I think it's best you stay out of things now. You know, lie low, don't ask questions."

I turned off a back street and onto the main road that

would take me straight to the animal shelter. "What do you mean?"

I heard papers rustling on his end. "I mean you don't need to be involved in this. It's dangerous, and I shouldn't have asked you to look into any of it." He coughed. "Besides, Jake's been released, and there's really no need for you to be involved. There wasn't in the first place, and I apologize for dragging you into it."

"What? Why are you…what's going on? Is it because they did something to the pooch party turf area? Is that it?"

"Yes, and no. I've put you in a—"

"Max, maybe before I didn't have reason to be involved, but first of all, if I didn't want to look into it, I would have said no. I'm capable of making a decision for myself, and secondly, this is personal now. Whoever did that to the turf, least case scenario, was trying to make a point, and worst case, was trying to hurt the dogs or me. Whether I want to be involved or not, I am, and I'm not going to lie low."

He grunted. "Sam would never want you in any kind of danger."

"I know that, but Sam also knew that I was fully capable of taking care of myself, and that if someone messed with my family, my claws come out. These dogs are my family, and regardless of whether this is about me or them, it impacts them, and I'm going to do whatever I can to make sure they're safe, and they all have the opportunity to find loving homes."

Huh. I'd surprised even myself with the amount of passion in my feelings and my determination to get to the truth.

"I don't think it's a good idea," he said.

"And I respect your opinion, but I'm going to do what's necessary to keep my program going, Max. I hope you can understand."

He sighed. "I do, and I'm going to help you because someone has to keep an eye on you. It's what Sam would want."

"There's no need of course, but thank you."

"Are you on your way to the fairgrounds?"

"No, I'm heading to the shelter. I've got dogs to train and retrain. I'm setting up some new volunteers. If nothing, the training program has opened the eyes of people that want to volunteer, so the dogs are getting a lot of people time."

"That's excellent. You should be proud of what you're doing. Can I bring you by a coffee? It's been a while since I've been there, and it'll be good for the program to have a city council member supporting it."

"Especially since one has been verbal about basically killing off a part of it entirely. I'd love a coffee."

"Great. And we'll discuss that when I see you. Be there in a few."

Max beat me to the shelter, and he wasn't the only city council member to do that.

CHAPTER SIX

"Mr. Morring, what a pleasure to see you." Allie pushed her ears down and back and kept her body low to the ground. She was clearly not a fan of the man, and I trusted her judgment completely.

He nodded as a slick smirk appeared on his face. "Always a pleasure, Mrs. Kingston."

I grabbed my messages from my small box in the main office and went on with my business while Max, Rick and the shelter manager, Mary Aberdeen chatted.

Max followed me into the back room and handed me my coffee. "I had no idea he'd be here."

I nodded. "I didn't think that you did." I took a small sip of the hot liquid and thanked him. "This is perfect."

Sara, the front desk person that morning stepped into the back room with us. "Missy, we've got three volunteers here to train. Where would you like them to go?"

Bandit barked. He loved coming to the shelter, probably because he knew he wouldn't stay long, but he could visit and play with his buddies. "Here," I handed the controller for their collars to Sara. "Give this to them, tell them not to play with it, and have them take Allie and Bandit back to the covered turf area. I'll be there in a minute."

"Yes, ma'am."

"Thank you, Sara."

Max smiled as he watched her leave. "They really like what you're doing here, don't they?"

I gathered up a stack of collars and controllers for the other dogs and told him to follow me. "I think so, or at least I hope so. We've had great success with the dogs, and our adoption rates are through the roof. One day last month we were actually at capacity, so that's a good thing."

"To be at capacity is good?"

I held the door to the dog area open for him as we received a welcome barking chorus fit for royalty. "Max, we're usually well past our capacity, and desperately begging for fosters. It was a big thing, believe me. The dogs are adoptable for many reasons, but the training makes a huge difference, and the fact that these people take the time to invest in the free training for them to learn how to work with their adopted dogs is huge. It means they're committed, and when they're committed, they don't return dogs to shelters."

He nodded and spoke loudly over the dog chorus. "I knew we had a problem, but I didn't realize how big. I'm glad you're doing what you're doing. Can you show me how you train them?"

"We're heading there now." I pushed open the door for the turf area and greeted the volunteers. One of my regular trainers was there, and she went and got three more dogs so each dog had a handler.

"It takes time to work with them all, and some aren't ready yet. They're either too sick, haven't been evaluated, pregnant, or we're not sure how they'll behave with the group yet. It's a long process, but it's the best we've got." I handed him a controller from the small table in the area. "This button is for the dog, you click it on the command, after you've taught the dog what to do of course." I showed him the three different options for training; shock, light, and vibration. "A lot of people disapproval of the shock version, but many aren't aware of what it does or how it works."

"What do you mean? It shocks them, right?"

"Approved shock collars like these are designed to get a reaction from the animal, and they do. Now here," I showed him the knob to control the level of shock. "If someone cranked that up to one hundred, the dog is going to notice of course, but that's not how you do it, not really. When I trained Bandit, he wrongly assumed he was the alpha, and for him to listen to me, he needed to know his place in the pack, and more importantly, that I'm the alpha. I had to use shock at first at about twenty-five, but by the end of the first thirty-minute training, he followed commands without any shock, light, or vibration. I tried to start with vibration, but he wouldn't listen. I placed a collar on the table in his hand. "Here hold this and tell me what it feels like."

"Wait." He tossed the collar back onto the table. "You're going to shock me, aren't you?"

I laughed. "You spoil all my fun."

He cringed. "I'm not sure I'm sorry about that, either."

"The training is more successful than treat training. Treat training teaches a dog to expect a reward of a treat every time they provide a desired behavior, but what if you're walking your dog at the park and a deer crosses the path. Do you think a treat is going to stop some dogs from charging the deer?"

"Probably not."

"Exactly. This training teaches them to react a certain way without receiving an award. It teaches them that specific behaviors, like sitting, heeling, not jumping on people, those kinds of things, are expected when asked. And this training is quicker, too. It can take a few days or a few hours, and the dog knows how to respond. The best thing about it is that once they're trained, you really don't need to use the shock, you can use the light or the vibration, or simply put the collar on and the dog understands, and eventually, you won't need it in the house at all. I do recommend it be kept on when outside or around people, not for the people's safety as much as for the dog's safety, but that's an entirely different conversation."

He nodded. "You're doing a lot for these dogs. I had no idea."

"Max, we have a dog population problem, and fixing dogs so they don't have puppies isn't the only solution. We need to find homes for the dogs we've got, and ensuring a dog is trained opens doors to homes that wouldn't be opened otherwise. Some people may not approve of the collar training, but it's helping adopt out dogs, and we won't give them to any family we don't personally train ourselves and approve for adoption.

"You can't keep them all, either. You don't have enough land."

I smiled. "Maybe someday."

He watched as the head volunteer, a woman who'd gone through the training course, taught the new volunteers how to work the controller, and he laughed when she made each of them feel the shock at different levels. "That's funny in an inappropriate way."

"They need to understand what the dog feels to have compassion and be allowed to work with them. If they don't meet our guidelines for training, they're out."

He nodded. "I'm impressed, Missy."

"Thank you, and I intend to make sure it continues." I'd

said that because Rick Morring and the shelter manager had just walked out the door to the turf area.

"Missy, Councilman Morring here would like to view the training. He's excited about the program and what it can offer the residents here in town," Mary said.

I made eye contact with Morring, and I knew he was full of it. He was only there for ammunition to stop the program. "Hey," I blew the whistle I'd worn on a lanyard around my neck. "Everyone bring it in. We're taking a break."

Mary's smiled disappeared.

I stared directly at Rick Morring. "Mary, our councilman here isn't interested in anything but removing the pooch parties from local events. He told me that himself, and I won't provide him access to a program he wants to destroy. And since this isn't a county shelter, and we don't rely on funding from the city government which employs him, I see no reason to allow him access to the program."

"I uh…I can't believe that's true. He's just finished telling me what a blessing it's been to have so many dogs adopted out since you came on board with the program," she said.

I still hadn't taken my eyes off Rick. "I know for a fact it is. Why don't you tell her what you said, Mr. Morring? Perhaps she'll have a better understanding."

His eyes bounced from me to Mary and then to Max before he finally said. "I came here today to learn more about the program with the hopes that I would leave feeling assured our community is safe where the dogs are present."

Mary twisted the cross on her thin silver necklace. "Mr. Morring, I can assure you the dogs Missy brings to town events have been well adjusted to people. I don't believe anyone is at harm. Of course, like any animal, precautions are made, and we do our best to ensure the safety of the community and our dogs." Her upper lip curled a bit on the right side, and I was happy to see Mary had similar feelings about the man as I.

Max placed his hand on Rick's shoulder and attempted to ease his concerns. "Rick, take a look around." He pointed to the dogs running around the turf park. "They're having a great time, and they aren't a threat to us at all. I'm confident Missy and her team take precautions when the dogs are out and about. In fact, I've seen it myself, and I'm pretty sure you have, too."

"It only takes one incident for the city to be held liable."

Mary pushed her shoulders back and stood tall. "We have permission and the necessary permits for every event we've participated in, Mr. Morring. We also have the insurance necessary to accommodate the requirements for such events, and should anything happen, which is unlikely, we are prepared to handle it."

Rick nodded. "Very well. Let's see how this next event goes. I'll be on hand to evaluate, and we'll go from there."

I fixed my eyes on him. "Lovely. I'm looking forward to spending time with you at the festival, Mr. Morring." I'd strained my neck so much while trying to keep my cool, I'd practically spit out his name, and if it was obvious, I didn't care one bit.

Since I had no other choice but to work with the volunteers and dogs in Rick's presence, we did, but I limited the training to an introduction for the volunteers, mostly showing what would be achieved through Bandit's example.

In my business, people like Rick Morring were the enemy, and I didn't want to share my secrets and give him ammunition to use them against me.

It felt like hours passed until Rick left, but he'd really only been there another forty minutes tops. Time dragged when I had to spend it with people I didn't respect, and I'd done my best to ignore him. Max stuck around, keeping himself busy speaking with other volunteers, helping clean the kennels, walking a few of the dogs, and engaging with people who'd come for adoption. As I headed back to the front office, I saw him sitting on the couch in the cat lounge with two fluffy, fat cats on his chest, one on his lap, and two others resting on each of his shoulders. I snuck in and none of them gave up their prime spots or even budged when I did. I snapped a photo for our adoption wall because it was just so adorable, seeing him lying there under a pile of cat fluff. When Max snored, I giggled and left him there, praying he didn't have an allergy because if he did, the poor guy would be miserable in minutes.

When the cat screeching volume rose, a few of us rushed out of the office to check, and there was poor Max, a cat on his head and one on two legs on his thighs. He held his arms up as if held a gun point, a frozen look of fright plastered on his face.

I couldn't help it, I laughed.

Mary pounded her fist on the lounge's large picture window, and the two cranky cats' heads pivoted toward us, and then they bounded off Max and went to their respective corners with their gang mates. Max practically jumped off the couch, and as he did, cat hair flew off his nice cream colored dress shirt, leaving a cloud of hair slowly falling to the ground.

I chuckled. The poor man. He obviously had no idea how territorial cats could be.

He exited the cat lounge and tried to brush off the remaining hairs from his shirt. "Well, I've always hoped two women would fight over me, but I'd have preferred they each have two legs."

I pressed my lips together and raised my eyes to the ceiling. I couldn't look at him because I didn't want to bust out laughing.

Mary had walked into the office and returned with a hair removal brush. She handed it to him. "We love having people hang out with the kitties, but next time you should wear something you don't mind getting full of hair."

He ran the brush up and down his shirt, and when he turned around, Mary and I giggled.

He completed the rest of a full circle to face us again. "What?"

I held out the hand for the brush. "Here. You've got a little on your back, too." A little was an understatement. Even though the volunteers cleaned the cat furniture often, with a room filled with kitties, it was impossible not to leave with Maine Coon sized amounts of hair on our bodies.

It took me a good two minutes to get most of the hair off. He wasn't cat hair free, but I did my best. I walked him to his car. "So, you didn't come here just to bring me a coffee."

He laughed. "No, I didn't."

"Well?"

"I talked to a contact at the department, and they don't see Rick as the killer."

I blinked. "So, what does that mean, they don't have any suspects?"

He shrugged. "The official word is they are diligently working the investigation, and the chief is planning to have a press conference with the mayor in a day or two."

I leaned against his car. "If they don't have a suspect, why would they have a press conference? Wouldn't that just make them look bad?"

"The wolves are circling, and the mayor's getting nervous.

We've had the three Atlanta news networks here asking questions. He's told the chief he's got twenty-four hours to give him something."

"Or?"

He shrugged again.

"So, if Fielding isn't a suspect, and Morring isn't, they've got to have their eyes on someone."

"I was led to believe, off the record of course, they do. I just couldn't get a name."

I exhaled. "Does your contact think what happened to the turf is connected?"

"They're investigating."

"Is it even legal to buy the stuff? Wouldn't it be hard for someone to get it? It has to be the same person."

"No, it's not illegal, but it is strongly controlled. My contact says they've got a team of investigators scouring every outlet for purchases, but South Carolina isn't far, and since it's available there too, they've got to go there as well. It's also available online, so finding out where it came from could take weeks or months even."

"You can purchase cyanide on the internet? That's ridiculous."

He agreed.

"What're the odds of two people using the same controlled poison in a matter of twenty-four hours and at the same fairgrounds?"

"Slim to none, I'd assume."

"Me, too. Whoever killed Traci Fielding put those poisoned pumpkins on the turf, I'm sure of it. And they either wanted to make a point, or stop the pooch party event. My guess is they were coming after me and the dogs to stop us."

"I think you're right."

I tapped my pointer finger on the cleft of my chin while I

thought things through, and then I slowly moved it and pointed toward the shelter. "I'm going to check the volunteer records. Maybe they'll tell me something."

"That's a good start."

"Do you have a relationship with Gina Palencia?"

He jerked his head back. "Gina and me? No, of course not."

I shook my head. "I mean like a friendship or whatever. Not a romantic one."

He blushed. "Oh, well, yes, I guess. We have worked together on a few things. We get along."

I filled him in on what happened the night before. "She hears a lot, or well, I guess she could be making it up, but I really feel like she came to see me for a reason, and it wasn't just to give me taco soup, or chili, or whatever it was. Maybe you could check on how she's doing with the festival, offer your help, whatever, and try to get some information from her?"

"You didn't eat the taco soup, did you?"

I shook my head. "Dumped it down the sink. Everyone's a suspect in my eyes."

"Even me?"

"Not yet."

He nodded. "Good to know. Tell me exactly what happened when she came over."

So, I did.

The pups and I headed over to the festival. I'd been in contact with the artificial turf company, and they'd graciously offered to replace the turf at no cost and scheduled the delivery for the festival instead of my house or the shelter, making my life a whole lot easier. It wasn't too hard to put down, mostly just a hassle, and I appreciated the extra hands.

I met the delivery truck at the pooch party set up, and the kind men helped remove the crates the police left scattered around to lay the grass down. I sprayed everything off after they left, giving it a good washing to get rid of any dust that might bother the dogs.

As I dried off my hands, Jennifer Lee came by. "Hey, Missy, I can't believe what happened. Do you need any help getting set up again?"

I didn't, but I took advantage of the chance to talk with her. "That would be wonderful Jennifer, thank you."

She helped move the crates back to their locations and set up the water bowls. She stood in front of the crates and examined them. After a moment, she aligned them in a straight even line and then smiled.

I stood next to her. "Type A?"

"A little," she said, making the pinch symbol with her thumb and forefinger.

I nodded. "Me, too."

"Do you know if they've got any idea who did this?" She faced me. "Is it related to what happened to Traci Fielding?"

I shrugged. "I don't know much yet. I know the investigation is going into South Carolina, but that's about it."

"South Carolina? Really? Whatever for?"

"Apparently, you can purchase cyanide in stores, so they're going there to see if any has been purchased. It's strongly regulated from what I've heard."

She nodded. "You can buy it on the internet, too."

I tilted my head. "Yes, but I didn't know that until today."

"Oh." She shook her head. "Me neither. I heard Jim Decon discussing it a little while ago."

"Really? With whom?"

"He was talking to one of the city council members. Rick Morring, I think."

"He sure seems to get around." I wanted to discuss her arguments with both Jake and Traci Fielding, but I didn't want to sound accusatory. I also wasn't sure Jennifer was involved in Traci's murder or the poisoned pumpkins in the pooch party area, but I wasn't about to lead her to believe I thought she was.

"As do a lot of the men in town."

Bingo! She'd just given me exactly the opening I needed, or at least one I could work with.

We were wiping down the crates and I stopped to face her. "May I ask you a question?"

She pursed her lips and then said, "Is this about me and Jake?"

I raised my eyebrows and angled my head to the right.

Jennifer sat on the turf. "It was stupid, and it was wrong, and I shouldn't have fallen for his lies. I admit that now, but I believed him. I couldn't help myself."

"Jennifer, people have seen you basically threaten him. If the police haven't talked to you yet, I'm sure they will. I don't want to sound accusatory, because that's not my intention."

"I know, and they have." She got back to wiping down a crate. "I'm sure he threw me under the bus the second he opened his mouth."

"So, where do you stand with police now?"

"I've been asked not to leave town." She threw the cloth onto the ground and cried. "I guess I'm a suspect."

"Do you have an attorney?"

She laughed. "Not everyone has your kind of cash. What I do have is my innocence, and that's what's important."

I wasn't sure I believed her, but she had looked me straight in the eyes when she claimed her innocence so that was something. "Jennifer, I saw you talking with Traci shortly before she was killed, and I had to tell the police. I didn't hear what you were talking about, but it was pretty clear you were arguing."

She sighed. "It's okay. I would have done the same in your shoes. You're right, we were arguing."

"May I ask what about?"

"I'd tried to apologize. I thought I owed her that, but she didn't want to hear it. She was angry, and I got defensive. It wasn't how I'd wanted things to go, and I told that to the detective. Bruno, I think?"

I could imagine how Traci might have reacted. Sam had always been faithful, there was no question about it, but if he wasn't, and the woman wanted to apologize to me, I don't think I would have reacted graciously. "That must have been a complicated conversation for both of you."

She nodded. "I've made my peace with my actions, and I can assure you, it won't happen again. No more married men for me. I learned my lesson."

I hoped that was true, but from what I understood, dating a married man was less about the fact that he was married and more about the woman herself. I wasn't a psychologist, and it had been years since I'd taken that Psychology 101 class in college, but as an avid reader, I'd run across articles and papers on the subject. I said a prayer of thanks for the life I'd been blessed to have. "What do you think happened to Traci?"

She stared at me for a moment. "I don't know, but if her murder and the poison here, if they're connected, then I think it's less about Traci and more about you."

I flinched, not because what she said sounded ludicrous, because it sounded realistic. "I'm inclined to agree with you, and I'm planning to find out what's going on."

CHAPTER SEVEN

My daughter sat on the couch in my keeping room, her head buried into her phone.

"Hayden? What're you doing here?"

Allie and Bandit greeted her with licks and butt wiggles.

"Hey, Mom, nice to see you, too."

I set a bag of groceries on the counter. "It's always nice to see you, of course, but it's unusual to see you without a call first."

She placed her phone on the coffee table and gave each dog ear scratches. "Allie's a cutie. Ferocious, for sure," she said after Allie swiped her long tongue up Hayden's face.

"Yes, she'll lick you to death if you're not careful."

"A horrible way to go."

"I was planning to make a salad for dinner. Would you like some? There's enough for two."

"Sure." She came to the kitchen and sat at the bar.

"So, spill it."

"What? Can't a daughter surprise her mother with a visit?"

"Not unless they're up to something or want money, and I'm pretty sure you don't want money."

She flipped her phone over and over. Hayden was like her father. She busied her hands when choosing the right words. "A friend from high school called and said your pooch party spot on the fairgrounds was vandalized, and I knew if I called you, you'd brush me off, so I decided to come out."

"A friend from high school?" There was only one friend from high school that would even consider calling Hayden and telling her anything, and that was her high school and college boyfriend, someone I didn't think she'd talked to in over a year. "Justin called you?"

She squirmed in her seat. "We've been talking some lately."

I hurried around the kitchen counter and planted my bottom onto the stool next to her. "You and Justin are talking again? Tell me everything."

She dipped her head and sighed. "Your kid comes here starving and all you want to do is gossip?" She flicked her head toward the salad I'd left in my excitement to know what happened. "I'll make you a deal. We eat and you tell me what's going on here, and I'll fill you in on some of what's going on with me."

I returned to the other side of the bar and finished mixing the salad while Hayden set the counter. She poured us each a glass of water.

"Some of what's going on?" I complained. "Tit for tat, you know. You share your secrets, I'll share mine. That kind of thing."

She dished salad onto each of our plates. "That's not how it works."

I smiled as I sat next to her. "That is one hundred percent how it works. Well, actually, you're right. It doesn't. As the mom, I should know more. My life is private." I tried to hold back my smile to no avail.

Her tone switched from casual to serious. "Justin said you could have died. Twice now in a matter of days. You have to be careful, Mom."

"Justin's exaggerating, and I am careful."

"He's a police officer. He's not exaggerating, and you know it. He said they found cyanide on the smashed pumpkins just like they did where the woman was killed." She placed her hand on my forearm and squeezed. "I'm worried. You're not getting yourself in over your head, are you?"

I all but spit my salad out in her face as I laughed almost uncontrollably. "That's the funniest thing I've heard in weeks. Me, in over my head."

She groaned. "It's the furthest thing from funny I've heard in weeks, and I'd appreciate it if you'd stop trying to change the subject. Please, tell me what's going on. I meant it when I said I'm worried."

From the look in her eyes, I knew she was, and I didn't want to push that under the rug. She'd already lost one parent, and I knew the fear of losing another weighed heavily on her heart. I held her hand. "Honey, I'm fine, and I promise, I'm going to stay that way."

She pressed her lips together and her eyes glossed over, so I hugged her. "Please, tell me what's going on," she said.

I explained everything but it didn't relieve her fears. In fact, it increased them.

"Mom, maybe you should pull out of the festival. Give things some time to blow over."

I finished chewing a bite of my salad. "Honey, I can't do that. I have a responsibility to the dogs and the shelter, and the program is going so well. I don't want to lose momentum."

"If something happens to you, you'll lose more than momentum."

"I've got it under control. You don't have to worry about me, Hayden. I promise."

"It's my job, especially since Dad isn't here to do it."

I hated how she'd taken on adult problems that didn't belong to her. Sam would have hated that, too. "No, your job is to live your life and not fear what might happen to me."

She half-smiled. "Because that's what you do with me?"

"It's different. You're my child."

"And you're my mom. It's not different at all."

She did have a point, at least from a daughter's view. "How about this? I've got to keep my dogs safe, and my program going, so I'm going to find out who's doing this because I know it has something to do with the pooch parties, but I promise you, I'll do my best to stay safe."

"And you'll text me daily to let me know you're okay?"

"Every night when I go to bed."

She smiled. "Just like Dad had me do my freshman year at Kennesaw."

Sam had made her do that her first year away for college. It broke his heart even though it swelled with pride that his little girl was accepted into the honors program there, a mere hour away. For Sam though, it felt like a thousand miles. "Yes, like Dad had you do freshman year."

I watched as a tear fell from her eye, and I silently promised her again I wouldn't let anything happen to me.

After Hayden left, I snuggled with the dogs in bed and perused the internet for information. The problem was, I didn't have a clue what I was looking for.

I searched for Jim Decon, hoping that would lead me to his articles about the pooch parties, and it did. There were twelve articles about the program, interviews with adoption families, myself, and various people in the community. One of them being Traci Fielding.

It wasn't exactly an interview about the program but about the festival. Traci mentioned the various events included, and the pooch parties got excellent exposure, though something she'd said gave me pause.

"I am most excited about the pooch party event," Fielding said. "Though there are some who feel this program is a potential hazard to the community, I disagree. It's a wonderful opportunity for citizens to experience the work our shelter is doing to help these sweet dogs find forever homes, and the program founder, Missy Kingston, works diligently with the dogs to train them and give them the skills necessary to be excellent additions to any local family. Regardless of what some members of city council think, the program is an excellent addition to the festival."

I'd missed that article when it published last week, which was unusual, especially because Jim Decon usually sent me the link after it went live. I wondered why he hadn't with that one.

Our city council meetings minutes as well as videos of them were always available online, so I went to the city website and searched the files. I could access each meeting's agenda and scan through them to see if anything about the pooch parties, the shelter, or the festival was on the schedule, and I found two incidents where they were.

I opened the first document and read through the minutes, finding a few scraps of information about the festival, but nothing out of the ordinary. I saved the page and went onto the next, where the minutes led me to view the video.

I watched, and though a part of me was surprised, overall,

I chastised myself for not addressing any of this prior to setting up the pooch party program in the first place.

A group of residents expressed their concern for the program, saying the dogs would be attractive to children, but because no one was sure of their emotional scars or how they were raised—misinformation for a good eighty percent of the dogs—they feared the children were at risk of injury and possible death, and they wanted the program eliminated from the festival entirely. I recognized most of the group, many of whom I knew personally, but seeing Gina Palencia there, listening to her express her personal concern for the welfare and safety of festival attendees threw me for a loop, a big, twisted loop.

Traci Fielding was there too, arguing in support of the program, citing a list of reasons that made me wish I could have thanked her for before she was killed.

Rick Morring supported the idea of eliminating the program and motioned to place it on the council docket with urgency.

Thankfully, the mayor disagreed, noting his reasons were Traci's explanation and his own children expressing their excitement about the event. Granted, he'd brought his kids to the shelter, and they'd spent many hours playing with the dogs and volunteering. He'd said he wanted them to learn about the benefits of volunteering, and the shelter was one of two places they'd go to regularly. His children never had any incident with the animals, and he spoke kindly of the program.

Max motioned to table the discussion, and another council person seconded the motion while Rick Morring's neck stiffened.

He desperately wanted the program shut down, and I wondered still if he'd go as far as murder to make it happen.

The next morning, I followed my normal routine then

dropped the dogs off at the shelter so they could play and headed to Atlanta Bread to meet Max. I'd texted him and offered to buy him a bagel and coffee.

"I watched a city council meeting about the pooch party program last night. Why didn't you tell me Morring wanted to officially shut it down?"

"Because it got killed, and I don't think it's going to happen."

"But in light of recent events, he's definitely a suspect now, don't you think? And Gina Palencia? She wanted to nix it too?"

He sighed. "I didn't understand that either. Maybe she's afraid of dogs?"

"She didn't really seem to be at my house the other day. Why would she be so adamant about it at the meeting? What's in it for her?"

"Maybe that's what we need to find out?"

I swirled the last bit of coffee in my mug. "You can bet I intend to do that today. She has done nothing but support the program to my face, so for her to want it killed is surprising."

"Be careful, Missy. I don't want you getting in over your head."

"Has the press conference been scheduled?"

"Not yet. The mayor sent a message to several of us last night saying they are close to an arrest, so he wants to wait."

"Did he mention who?"

He shook his head.

"It's got to be Gina or Rick. It has to be. Both of them wanted the program ended."

"I don't think this is about the pooch parties, Missy."

"Of course it is. They both wanted them shut down, and Traci didn't, and now she's dead, and they tried to get me, too."

"The police think you were a distraction for them, that it was about Traci, and doesn't have anything to do with you or the dogs."

I leaned back in my seat. "No, no. That's not right. This is about the dogs. I'm sure of it."

"I'm not sure anymore."

"Well, I am, and I intend to prove it."

He exhaled. "I knew you were going to say that."

I gathered my things and stood. "Of course you did. I've got to go. I'd like to talk to someone before I head to the fairgrounds."

"Would you like me to come?"

I shook my head. "I'm good, but thanks."

I drove to the police department and asked to see Lieutenant Johns.

The front desk officer behind the glass smiled. "He's in a meeting at the moment, but it should be ending soon. Would you like to wait?"

"Yes, thank you."

He nodded. "I'll send him a quick text to let him know you're here. Your name?"

"Missy Kingston."

A few minutes later, Justin, Hayden's ex, stepped out from the locked door to greet me. "Mrs. Kingston, I had a feeling I'd see you today." He gave me a welcoming hug.

"I bet you did, and at what point am I going to convince you to stop calling me Mrs. Kingston? That's my mother in law, God rest her soul."

Justin laughed. "Let's go back to one of the conference rooms. I'm sure you have a lot to talk about." He glanced at my purse. "You don't have a gun in there, do you?"

I smiled. "Actually, I do."

He laughed. "Of course you do. Mr. Kingston trained you well."

I opened my purse and handed him my Sig Sauer, which he slid through the window to the front desk officer for safe keeping. "Put that in the drawer for me, will you?" he asked.

The man nodded at Justin and smiled at me. "Nice choice."

I returned the smile and said thank you.

Sam purchased the gun for me two years before he died. He'd signed me up for classes to learn how to use it properly and ever since, I've made a habit of going to the range to practice and improve my skills. Since his passing, I felt the need to be able to protect myself with or without a weapon and had begun taking self-defense courses, and in the past year, started a jujutsu class where I'd done well. Being older and alone, one must be prepared, and I wanted to make sure I was.

In the conference room, Justin pulled out two chairs next to each other and offered one to me. "Am I going to get lectured?"

I laughed. "You did worry my daughter needlessly, but it was with good intentions, so I understand."

"It wasn't needlessly. You could have been killed, and I knew she'd want to know. I also knew you'd be the last one to tell her."

He wasn't incorrect. "But that should have been my decision."

He nodded. "Yes, but I don't care. You're like a second mom to me."

"If you'd get your butt in gear, I could be your mother in law."

It was his turn to laugh. "We'll discuss that another time, and I'll try to call you Missy. Now tell me how I can help you."

"I heard the department is close to an arrest for Traci Fielding's murder?"

He leaned back in his chair and exhaled. "That's often something chiefs say when they want to buy time."

"So, you're not?"

"I can't officially say, but I have some thoughts."

"Okay. I can respect that." I removed my purse from my lap and placed it on the table. "Is it your opinion that the poisoned pumpkins on the turf were a way to distract the killer's real intent?"

He inhaled and held the breath as he chose his words. "Mrs. Kingston—"

I narrowed my eyes at him.

"Missy. Yes, I worry that this may involve you in some way, but the only thing tying the two incidents together is the cyanide, but until they find more evidence, it's just a feeling."

I sat up straight in my seat. "That's what I think, and I think Rick Morring and Gina Palencia are involved."

He raised his right eyebrow. "You think a councilman is involved in Traci Fielding's murder?"

I nodded.

He glanced at the window into the room and then he stood. "How about I walk you to your car?"

"But I wanted to ask you—"

"It's nice outside. I'm cooped up in here. I could use the fresh air." He guided my elbow with his hand.

We stepped outside. "This isn't the right place to have this discussion. Can we meet later to talk?" he asked.

"The police department isn't the right place to discuss a murder?"

He shrugged. "Not when you're accusing a city councilman of it, no." He pressed his hands together in a prayer-like position. "There are alliances here. People that support certain government officials, have mutually beneficial relationships, and the walls have ears. You have to watch your accusations. They could be used against you."

"All the more reason to look into my theory."

"Exactly what is your theory about Morring?"

I told him what I'd learned. That Rick Morring tried to get Traci to cut the pooch party, that he'd suggested it at a city council meeting, and that Gina Palencia supported it at the meeting while Traci Fielding told him she had every intention of keeping the party as planned.

I continued on. "And Rick tried to act like he didn't disapprove of the parties. He lied to my face about it, but I finally got him to admit his issues in front of the shelter manager and Max Hoover."

He stared at the ground. "That is suspicious."

"Exactly."

"I'm not making any promises, but I'll ask around, look into a few things and see what I can find out, okay?"

"I'd appreciate it."

"In the meantime, I want you to lie low. Stay out of Morring's way. If he is involved, the last thing you need is to tick him off."

"What about Gina Palencia? Will you look into her?"

He groaned. "I've not heard a negative thing about her, but yes, I'll ask around, see if anyone's had troubles with her."

I nodded. "You'll let me know if you find out anything?"

"Yes, ma'am. It's the least I can do. Hayden needs you. It's my duty to keep you safe for her."

"You still have feelings for her, don't you? I knew it."

He blushed, but I didn't call him out on that. "I'll always care for your daughter. She was an important part of my life. I wouldn't be where I am today without her."

"She feels the same."

I left the station and headed straight for the fairgrounds

but decided to take a detour and stopped at the shelter instead. I picked up Bandit and Allie and took them with me.

I wasn't the kind of person to back down from a battle, especially one that meant so much to me, and I knew one of the ways to dispel any concern over the animals at the festival was to get them out in front of people. I organized a quick training session at the fairgrounds with two of the volunteers and two other dogs. Each of the volunteers drove separately with their assigned dog.

Initially they were assigned what I liked to call an event wander, where each dog walked the entire festival grounds—on leash—with a trainer to meet and greet prospective adopters. It wasn't something we did often because we had so many dogs, but we did sometimes pick a few well trained ones to show off. It always worked. Those dogs were adopted every single time. Since the festival wasn't set to open for a few days, it was perfect practice for both dogs and trainers, and a great option to get a feel for those in the trenches and their reactions to the dogs. I wanted to find out who might be on Team Rick.

While the pack was out, I took Bandit and Allie on a wander also, but I used their electronic collars and no leather leash. If anyone showed signs of issue or concern, I'd add them to my list.

I wanted my list to shink, but if anyone with a negative or uncomfortable reaction could be connected to Rick or Gina, I'd be happy.

As we rambled around the fairgrounds, I kept my eyes out for Gina, Jennifer, and Rick. Several volunteers, exhibitors, and festival staff were thrilled to see the dogs and stopped to chat us up, giving me the perfect opportunity to ask questions. Not one of them showed anything but excitement about the program, and my heart warmed.

"So, how's it going now? I'm sure Gina's got everything under control, right?" I asked two festival staff members.

The male nodded. "Gina? She's the best. Don't think we'd a got better under the circumstances."

The woman's upper lip twitched, and I knew I'd get a different opinion from her. "It's just awful, what happened to Traci, and I don't want to sound ungrateful, but I sure wish someone else would have taken the job instead."

"Now sweetie, you know it's wrong to speak ill of people like that." He tugged on her sweater. "God don't like that."

She jerked her arm away from his grasp. "God don't like nobody with an ego the size of Texas neither, and that Gina Pal-however you say it, she's got just that."

I pushed for more. "I'm sorry, did something happen?"

"Girl just thinks she owns the festival. Thinks she can step in and do whatever she wants. Why, she changed the entire layout of the food trucks on a whim. Said she preferred them at the front of the lot instead of spread throughout, and that's just stupid. People don't got no reason to walk the full festival if there ain't food in the back, 'least in my opinion."

She had a point. "Did anyone argue that point?"

She nodded. "A few of us spoke up, but she said it's the way it is, and nothing is goin' to change it. She's wanting to move you too, but don't see how that's gonna work since you had the new grass put out and all."

Gina wanted to move the pooch party area? "Where was she looking to move me?"

"To the back. Told everyone is would eliminate the risk of them dogs of yours hurting attendees. I told her those dogs ain't the problem. People are the problem, just like them commercials say."

I thanked them both and went on a search for Gina. I was livid, and I was surprised I couldn't see the steam coming out from my ears because it sure felt like my head was going to explode.

I kept the dogs heeled closely to my sides and walked the entire fairgrounds in search of her and finally found her just before I'd about given up, back in a corner near the permanent restrooms on the far end of the lot.

With Jake Fielding's hands holding onto her at the waist.

"Well look at that," I said to the dogs. "Not at all what I expected to see."

Allie wagged her tail, but Bandit wasn't all that interested in Jake's affairs. He'd spotted a small box turtle on the ground and was afraid to move.

Bandit feared frogs and box turtles because, you know, they were so vicious. I patted his bum and giggled. "Bandit, what's it going to do, jump out of its shell and attack your nose?"

He kept silent, and Allie joined in on his curiosity, which gave me ample opportunity to catch a few words of the interesting couple's conversation.

CHAPTER EIGHT

Justin chewed something while I listened on the other end of the line. "You heard what?" The munching and chomping sound made me cringe.

"Have you forgotten your manners?"

He stopped. After a few seconds of silence, which I assumed were used to swallow down whatever he'd been eating, he apologized. "Not everyone has a chance to take a meal break, and there's been a murder, so suffice it to say, it's been a busy week."

I felt bad for giving him a hard time. After all, he was trying to help me. "I know. I'm sorry. What I said was I heard Jake Fielding and Gina Palencia in a—" I paused to find the right words. "Talking in a compromising position."

"I'm going to need a little more than that, Mrs.—Missy."

"He had his hands on her waist, and not in an aggressive way. I couldn't hear everything they said because I was too far away, but I think I heard him tell her she was doing a great job, and he'd thank her…" I paused again. "In a way she'd enjoy immensely or something like that." I shuddered as a strong sense of ick filled my gut. I wasn't into public displays of affection at all, and between two people that could be involved in a murder just upped the ick factor miles high.

"Did you hear anything specifically related to the pooch parties or the poisoning?"

I sighed. "No, I didn't."

"They could have been talking about anything. If you want them brought in, Bruno's going to need more than a sketchy conversation. And he's already cleared Fielding."

"But he hasn't cleared Gina. Maybe they're lovers and she's doing his dirty work? Or maybe she wanted Traci out of the picture?"

"I can mention it to Bruno, but I can't guarantee he'll do anything with it." He coughed. "Other than tell you to stay out of his investigation."

"I'm not in his investigation. I was merely walking through the fairgrounds and saw something questionable between two people directly involved with a murder victim. It's my duty as a citizen to inform the police."

"You can swing it any way you want, but you're saying the same thing I am."

He was right. "So, what do I do?"

"Ideally, you should let the police do their job, but I have a feeling that's out of the question."

"Justin, whoever killed Traci Fielding tried to kill me, too. I don't question that. The incidents weren't separate, and if the police don't put it together, then someone has to."

He exhaled. "Let me dig into Gina a little further. I'll see if she has a history of, I…I don't know. Just a history, I guess. I'll get back to you."

"Thank you."

"In the meantime, do me a favor and keep your head down and as far away from this as possible, please? For

Hayden's sake. Like I've said a few times already, she can't lose you."

"Understood."

After we hung up, I thanked God that Hayden had someone watching over her.

Two hours later, Justin texted and asked to meet me. Since I was still at the fairgrounds, he said he'd come there. Less than ten minutes later, he was at the pooch party section, dressed in his police uniform.

He sat next to me, and I raised my eyebrow. "Don't you think you coming here in a professional capacity will look suspicious?"

"Why? Your event was vandalized, and I'm here following up." He pushed his chair closer to mine and watched as Allie and Bandit ran around the turf playing with a ball. "I pulled up some interesting information on that person you asked about."

"Do tell."

"Seems she's had some issues in her previous state."

"Really? What kind of issues?"

Bandit brought him the ball and he tossed it across the turf. Both dogs went running, but Allie ran past it, not interested in getting the ball, just having fun running for it and distracting Bandit.

He leaned onto the back of the chair and tilted his body toward me. With his arms casually folded across his chest, he spoke softly. "Two 9-1-1 calls for domestic disturbances, but no charges filed."

"What happened?"

"Looks like it was a boyfriend. Accused her of hitting him and threatening to poison him."

My eyes widened. "Are you serious?"

He nodded.

I fought back the urge to jump up and cheer. "So, what do we do? Did you talk to the detective?"

"He's meeting us here."

As he said that, I glanced around my circle of vision, but I didn't see Detective Bruno anywhere. "When?"

He checked his watch. "Five minutes. But before he gets here, I need to prepare you. He's not going to be happy I've told you. It's his investigation, not mine."

"But if it helps to solve a murder, what does it matter?"

"Telling a citizen about a possible connection in a murder investigation goes against policy. And I should have given him a heads up that I was looking into her."

"Can you get in trouble?"

He shook his head. "It's an active investigation. It's just not mine. It wasn't cool, but I out rank him, so if he takes his ego out of it, it should be fine."

"I'll take responsibility. Tell him I pressured you to help me."

He laughed. "If I fall to the pressure of a local dog shelter volunteer, I shouldn't be a cop, let alone a lieutenant."

He had a point.

Bruno stepped into the pooch party area, and I bounded from my seat to greet him. "Detective, I…I…Justin was just trying to—"

Justin stood and stopped me from very likely making the situation worse than it was. "Bruno, I came across some information you should know."

We discussed what Justin had discovered, and to my surprise, Detective Bruno wasn't upset. He made direct eye contact with me. "Why didn't you come to me with your suspicions?"

"I wanted to but honestly, you're not the easiest person to be around," I said without any hesitation.

Justin coughed.

Bruno nodded. "You're not the first person to say that, ma'am."

Justin laughed out loud that time, and I smiled, then I relayed my recent experiences with Gina to the detective and Justin told him what he'd found.

Bruno asked me if I'd noticed anything about Gina when I saw her, but I wasn't sure what he meant.

He tipped his head back and checked behind him. "What she was wearing? Her body language with Mr. Fielding?"

I closed my eyes to create an image, but I couldn't come up with anything. "I'm sure she's still here. I could try and text her if you'd like?"

He shook his head. "No need. I'll make my rounds and see if I can find her."

Justin said, "Less suspicious that way."

I nodded.

"Mrs. Kingston, I appreciate you providing information, but I don't want you doing anything that might get you hurt. There's already been a threat to your life. You need to stay out of the investigation."

"So, you think it was a threat against me?"

"We're treating it as such whether it was or not. I can't say for sure, but I can ask that you keep out of my investigation."

"You can't say they aren't either. In fact, you just said—"

"I'm aware of what I just said. For now, I ask that you do what you must to keep yourself safe, and stay away from those who might be suspects in a murder."

Justin faced me. "Missy, he's right. You need to be careful. Let the police handle it from here."

I shifted my weight from one foot to the other. "It's

getting late. I've got to get to the shelter." I nodded at the two men. "Thank you for your concern."

I called the pups over, made sure their collars were secure, and we all headed to my car. On my way out, I ran into Jake Fielding.

"Missy." He smiled, and it made my stomach churn in an unpleasant way. "How's the dog event coming along? You ready for the festival?"

I nodded. "I'm surprised to see you here considering…"

He flinched. "I've been cleared as a suspect, and I thought it my duty to make sure Traci's event, one she'd worked hard to make a success, stayed true to her goals."

I laughed. "Really? You want to help the woman you're cheating on, the woman you wanted to divorce?"

His eyes darkened. "You don't know the nature of our relationship, Mrs. Kingston."

"Maybe not, but I do know you're the last person Traci would want ensuring the integrity of her event." I made sure to look him straight in the eye. I wasn't one hundred percent sure of what Traci would have wanted, but I had a strong feeling I was right because it's what I would have wanted in the situation.

"That may be true, and perhaps this is my way of making amends."

"If that works for you."

"Mrs. Kingston, you think I killed my wife, don't you?"

"My thoughts are none of your business."

"Of course, but I can assure you, as I have before, I did not kill Traci, and I certainly didn't smash those poisoned pumpkins on your turf. I have no issue with you."

"Tell me, were you sleeping with Gina Palencia before Traci died, or is that something new?"

He winced. "My private life is of none of your concern."

"I'll take that as a before. And Mr. Fielding, let me just say this. If you're doing something to stop my pooch party program, if you're in any way involved in that, I'll do whatever's necessary to stop you."

He raised an eyebrow. "Is that a threat?"

I smiled. "If you're not involved, then no."

"Mrs. Kingston, I have no problem with your little shelter program. In fact, I've told Gina it's a great idea, and she shouldn't be worried about it being an issue at the festival."

I didn't believe him, but that didn't matter. I needed to stop talking before I said something I shouldn't. "Have a nice day, Mr. Fielding." As I turned to leave, he stopped me with a tight grip on my upper arm. I jerked it away. "Keep your hands off me, Jake."

He pulled his arm back and held his hands up in front of his body. "Missy, you're right. Someone is trying to take down your program, but it's not Gina. Trust me on that."

∽

Jennifer Lee rushed up behind me as I maneuvered the dogs into my car. "Missy, wait up."

I flipped around and saw her breathing heavily. "Hi, Jennifer."

"I...I..." She paused and caught her breath. "I'm out of shape, that's what I am."

I smirked. "Dogs will change that up right away."

"Yes, I suspect they would." She held her hand toward the open hatch of my vehicle and let the dogs sniff it. "I saw you talking to Jake. Neither of you looked happy."

"I'm fine but thank you for your concern." I wasn't sure where she was going with the conversation, but I wasn't going to shut the door and let her think I was leaving. I wanted to see what she had to say.

"Have you heard anything else about Traci's murder? Is Jake a suspect still?"

"I don't really know. I'm not involved in the investigation." I had no intention of telling her anything.

"Oh, no. Of…of course not. I just thought maybe you'd been told something because of what happened to your section of the—"

"I don't know much. The police aren't telling me anything other than to watch my back."

"Do you think the two are connected?"

I examined her outfit. It was October, and while it wasn't exactly cold, in my opinion it was too late for open toed shoes, and it wasn't at all the environment for those things anyway. Jennifer didn't want to volunteer because she wanted to help the event, not dressed like a woman on the prowl at least. She was there for other reasons. I wondered if that was true of Gina and her fashionable attire, too? I knew she was fishing for information, and I wasn't going to give her anything. "I think I should leave it to the police to figure out."

I didn't want her to think I suspected her of anything, and realized my tone came off rude when she jerked her head back and narrowed her eyes. I dialed it back the best I could. "I'm sorry, Jennifer. I guess I'm just stressed out from all of this. It's scary, thinking it's possible someone wants me dead."

She placed her hand on my shoulder. "Oh, honey, I can only imagine. I'm sorry you're going through this. Hey, what're you doing tonight? How about I come by with a bottle of wine and we can chat? Say around seven o'clock?"

There was nothing less enjoyable for me than idle chit chat with a woman I barely knew and wasn't quite sure I liked. Hayden said I needed a tribe, but I didn't agree. Groups of women were fine in social settings, but I'd learned that women weren't a lot different than they were in junior high. Cliques established themselves everywhere, and I'd felt the thrill of being on top along with the burn of being left out. I wasn't comfortable in either. It was likely my mouth and my inability to keep it shut at the most important times, but I wasn't about to change. I have six versions of the *the more I know people, the more I like my dogs* shirt for a reason. But if Jennifer knew something, or if she was involved in any way, it could be my only chance to find out. "Sure, that would be great."

I offered her my address, but she declined. "I know where you live."

"Great. I'll see you tonight."

"I'll be there," she said, and went on with her business.

I had enough time to check on the dogs at the shelter, give them some much deserved love and treats—which I enjoyed more than them—and then rush back home to search the internet for Gina Palencia. I started my laptop and searched her name, but I wasn't going to pay for some cheesy background check that wouldn't get me anything. She had several social media accounts, and I was able to give those a cursory eye, but since I wasn't on any of them, I really didn't understand how they looked.

I'd downloaded the few pictures I'd been able to take over the past few days and stared intently at the shoe prints. I had no idea what I was looking for, and even less of a clue what the police did in that kind of situation. I thought about Gina, Jake, Rick, and Jennifer, and anyone else that might have a reason to kill Traci Fielding and hurt me. I couldn't come up with any concrete thoughts, but I did know not one of those people wore boots with a large square heel like the print in the photos.

Could it have been someone else entirely?

Allie snored loud enough to break her out of her instant slumber. Both dogs were exhausted, having spent the day in the fresh air, and since I'd fed them at the shelter, when we got home, they each dropped onto a fluffy dog bed in the keeping room and were out like lights in minutes.

I desperately wanted to change into a baggy sweatshirt and sweats, especially since Jennifer was dressed to impress earlier, but I didn't. I stayed in my dark jeans and burgundy sweater and tidied up our already clean kitchen waiting for her to show up.

Which she did, promptly at seven o'clock.

I answered the door with a fake smile plastered on my face. "Hey, come on in."

She stepped inside and handed me a bottle of cheap white wine. "I know it's not fancy, but it's actually one of the better ones I've had. I'm in this wine club, and I get all these fabulous wines that honestly taste like garbage. This one is a hundred times better."

I smiled. "It's fine. Sam and I used to drink wine from a box. He always said it was the people you drank with, not the cost of the bottle that mattered."

She nodded. "Smart man."

We stared at each other for a moment in that awkward we have nothing more to stay kind of way. I finally shifted my feet, closed the door behind her and headed to the kitchen. "Follow me. The dogs are crashed, so you don't have to worry about them."

"Oh, I'm not." She examined my house. "Wow, your home is beautiful. I'd love to live in something like this."

I unscrewed the bottle and poured us each a glass. "Thank you." I handed her one. "We like it."

She gave me a sad smile. "It must be hard."

I realized what I'd said. "Oh, I'm sorry. I'm just used to talking like a couple." I hesitated and laughed. "I don't even realize I'm doing it most of the time." I walked over to my gray sectional couch and moved my laptop over to the coffee table. "Let's sit."

She followed. "So, how are you doing with all of this? It must have been awful, finding Traci and then seeing someone had vandalized your area of the festival."

"I'm okay. It's business as usual for me. I've got to get everything ready, make sure the dogs we're bringing are up to speed with their training and all, so that's taken a lot of my time." While that was true, I hadn't exactly ignored what had happened. I just didn't think that was information she needed. I wasn't up for the additional prodding.

She placed her wine glass on the table and shifted her position on the couch. "Can I ask you what it was like, finding Traci?"

Basically, she just did. I gave her question some serious thought. "You know, I'm not sure how it felt. I saw her, and I did what I had to do. I don't even know if I thought it through. I just acted."

She nodded and relaxed her back. "Oh, well, I would have been a complete basket case, finding her like that." She continued to nod. "But I'm a hot mess when anything out of the ordinary happens." She reached for her glass and took a sip. "You were probably devastated to find the pumpkins smashed on the turf. And to discover they had cyanide on them." She waved her empty hand in the air. "That must have been awful."

"I just hope the police solve both cases quickly." I took that moment to turn the tables on her and see what I could find out. "Do you think the two are related?"

She pressed her lips together. "I mean, it would be quite a

coincidence to have two random people use the same type of poison, unless of course the person responsible for the pumpkins was just a copycat. I guess it would help to know if cyanide is easy to get. I wouldn't know anything about that, but I'm sure you've checked into it given the circumstances."

I raised an eyebrow. We'd had a similar discussion earlier and she'd said she knew it could be purchased over the internet. Had she forgotten, or was she lying? "Didn't you tell me earlier it could be bought on the internet?"

Her eyes widened. "Oh, gosh. Yes. I forgot about that. I'm all stressed out about this. I can imagine you must be, too. Do you think it was purchased on the internet?"

"I have no idea," I said, wondering what she was trying to accomplish.

"Oh. Well, I guess if someone wanted to, they could. I mean, desperation is a strong motivator."

"What makes you think they were desperate?"

"Because of the dogs, of course." She stood and walked over to our half wall of bookcases, eyed the various books, and then removed *The Art of War*. Flipping casually through the pages, and without looking at me, she said, "I've been thinking about it, and whoever killed Traci must have done it because of the pooch party. She'd pushed so hard to keep it part of the festival, and it's obvious to me that's what got her killed."

I straightened my back. "You think Traci's death is because of my dogs?"

She placed the book back on the shelf. "Don't you? Just hours before she died she was arguing with the festival powers that be to keep the pooch party there, and then the smashed pumpkins on your turf? Doesn't seem like a coincidence to me."

"You saw her arguing? With whom?"

She sat back on the couch. "Rick Morring."

I pressed my lips together.

"You do know he wants your program shut down, and poor Traci, she was determined to keep it up, at the festival at least."

I nodded. "I can't imagine she'd be killed over my event."

"You don't know, do you?"

"Know what?"

"What Rick's been doing? About the beer garden?"

I tilted my head. "Apparently not. Why don't you tell me?"

"That's what the argument was about. He wants to replace your event, at the festival at least, with one. He said it'll bring in hundreds of thousands of dollars for the city. Last year the festival brought in over a million dollars, but he thinks a beer garden will up that by at least half. Given that your dogs don't bring in a dime, he feels eliminating it is fine."

I had to force myself from not appearing shocked. It wasn't easy. "This is the first I'm hearing about a beer garden."

She shrugged. "Given my relationship with Traci, I didn't talk to her about it personally, but she wanted nothing to do with a beer garden, and she made that clear at the volunteer meetings. The festival has beer sellers already, and drinking is limited to certain parts, so she thought adding a beer garden would be more of a problem than it's worth."

"I imagine it could be a nightmare for the police."

She nodded. "That was her other issue. Encouraging people to drink may be good for city budgets, but it's not good for the community." She sipped the last bit of her glass of wine. "But your program, it's good for the community."

"And for the dogs. Did you hear all Morring say any of this to her?"

"With my own ears."

"Did you tell the police?"

She sighed. "No. I didn't think about it at the time, but I guess I should."

"You need to tell them. It could be important."

~

Jennifer spent another hour talking about the festival and then left. I finally had a moment to change into my comfy clothes but went for my pajamas over the sweats. I let the dogs out and sat on the couch, staring at my computer.

After thirty minutes of blank staring and deep thought, I abandoned my laptop on the couch and walked out to the gazebo. Sam and I used to stroll the property at night, and though it was safer with a man next to me, it was a tradition of sorts I wasn't willing to give up. The walking allowed me to think, gave me peace, and made me feel more connected to my late husband.

I wandered the property thinking about what Jennifer had said. Was it true that Rick Morring wanted a beer garden? If so, why hadn't that been mentioned in the council meetings? More than likely that would have required a permit or approval or something, so wouldn't he have mentioned it?

I checked the time on my phone, which I'd always carried with me while on the property. I'd been out for over an hour, and it was just past ten o'clock. Growing up, we weren't allowed to answer the phone after nine, but times had changed, and texting at any hour didn't appear to be an issue for most, so I decided to go ahead and text Max.

"Hey, I'm sorry if it's late, but are you aware that Morring wants to put a beer garden where the pooch party is?"

I watched as the three dots on the text message thread appear. "He mentioned it briefly, but that's it."

My thumbs went to town on my screen. "Why didn't you tell me?"

More white dots that took forever to become a message. "Because he dropped it."

"I don't think he did though. Traci was arguing with Morring about it before she was killed."

"Are you sure?"

"Yes." I'd sat in the gazebo as both dogs slept on the floor beside me. "He wanted to—Can you talk? It's easier than texting."

There were no dots, and when the phone rang, and Max's contact popped onto my screen, I quickly answered.

"Who told you this?"

"Jennifer Lee."

He was silent.

"Okay, I know what you're thinking. She's probably not the most reliable source, but she offered to come over with a bottle of wine, so I figured, why not, and that's when she told me."

His breath was heavy and long. "Tell me what she said."

I gave him the details, ticking them off like bullet points on a typed to do list. "She thinks Traci's death is because she didn't want the beer garden."

"He doesn't need her approval for it. It's a city run festival. Council makes the decisions."

I figured that, but I had a theory. "Sure, but Traci's been running the show for how many festivals now? If she was against it, she could have threatened to quit. That would have been an issue, don't you think?"

"Gina seems to be doing a decent job of managing it now."

"Because it's in the final stages. Traci handles it from day one, or she did. From planning to scheduling to execution, she was in charge of everything, and she'd already done most of it. What's to stop Morring from killing her and setting it up at the last minute? Cutting a large area like mine for a beer garden would be easy and it would definitely go over well with attendees. And what's the best way to make that happen?"

"Vandalize the pooch area so it's considered unsafe."

"Em."

He was silent for a moment. "Let me do some digging in the morning. Can we talk after breakfast?"

I headed back to the house, walking faster than the dogs because they'd done a lot of running earlier on their four legs than me with my measly two.

CHAPTER NINE

"It's the backdoor over here." I pointed to the door leading out to our deck from the keeping room. "They broke the window to unlock it," I told the police officer standing beside me.

He stepped toward the door carefully as Justin entered through the front of the house hollering, "Missy?" with panic in his voice.

"Back here," I replied.

He jogged into the room and gave it a quick examination. "You okay?"

I nodded. "We were at the gazebo. I didn't hear anything."

He pointed to the dogs on each side of my legs. "They didn't either?"

I shrugged. "They had full days. They were snoozing in the gazebo, and you know how far it is from the house."

He nodded. "Might want to keep one at home if you go out like that."

I shuddered at the thought of what could have happened to one of them if whomever had broken into my house saw them. Dogs couldn't protect themselves from bullets.

Justin studied the broken window on my door. "This is new, isn't it? The door."

I breathed in deeply. "You do pay attention to detail, don't you?"

"It's my job. The last door had small windows on the top. We had to knock to get in one night, and Hayden couldn't see inside them because she's too short."

I smiled at the memory. They'd walked to the end of the property, and Sam knew it was probably to do something neither of us would want to know about, so he decided it would be funny to lock the door and make things awkward for all of us. It was definitely awkward then, but a fun memory now. I smiled.

Justin did, too. "Mr. Kingston would have never approved a door like this. It's not safe, especially for a…" He let the rest of that sentence finish itself.

"I like the natural light that comes through." I shook off the discussion, saving it for a later date. "My laptop is missing."

When I'd come back with the dogs, I saw what I thought was a person running along the side of my house, but I wasn't sure until the dogs barked and took off running. I immediately commanded them to heel, and though Bandit did, Allie isn't as trained, and kept going. I went into panic mode and ran at full throttle with Bandit just ahead of me, chasing my dog to make sure she was safe over chasing after the person who'd been inside my home.

It might not make sense to a non-dog owner, but for me, I'd rather lose my personal belongings over my animals.

"Did you get a good look at the person?"

I shook my head. "Just their back. Short, under six feet, wearing all black, including a mask which covered the person's entire head. I'd left lights on outside, but the person was already rounding the corner of my house by the time I saw them."

"Tell me what happened."

I went through the details once again, since I'd already done it for the officer that had responded to my 9-1-1 call. "We stayed out of the house in case someone else was inside. I kept the dogs with me across the street and waited for your officer to arrive, and now we're here."

"And just the laptop was taken?"

"As far as I can tell."

A young man in khaki pants and a blue windbreaker with the city emblem on it, walked over to us. "We've got some footprints. I've taken photos of them. Do you want a mold?"

Justin nodded.

I asked Justin, "Do you know if they found any prints at the pooch party?"

"Only about two hundred. We've got people going through them all now."

Training dogs without knowing their history was hard, but that had to be next to impossible.

I'd noticed the prints outside and snapped photos of them with my phone, but they were hard to see with the flash.

Allie approached the man dusting the door for prints. She kept her head low. "Allie, it's okay. Place," I said, pointing to her dog bed near the couch.

She gave the man one last sniff and sulked as she walked to the bed. When she laid down, she groaned her frustrations.

"Maybe you should stay in a hotel tonight. I can board up the glass for you, but I think Hayden would be more comfortable if you weren't here."

I furrowed my brow. "Hayden doesn't know what happened, and I don't think the person that broke in will come back."

Max walked up behind me. When he said hello, I jumped. He smiled. "Sorry about that."

"What're you doing here?"

He glanced at Justin and then back at me. "Someone told me your house was broken into. I wanted to make sure you're okay."

I glared at Justin. "You haven't called Hayden, have you?"

"No, ma'am, but I think you should."

"I will, once everything is handled, at least. In the meantime, I'd appreciate it if you didn't say anything to her. She's got enough on her plate. She doesn't need to worry about me."

"You're her mother, she's going to worry about you," Justin said.

"Nonetheless, please let me tell her."

He nodded. "I've suggested Missy stay in a hotel, but she doesn't want to."

"What am I supposed to do with the dogs? I can't leave them here alone. What if the person comes back?"

Justin rolled his eyes. "You just said you didn't think they would."

"Well, I don't, but if they do, I don't want to leave my dogs here helpless."

The two men eyed each other and then Max dragged his fingers along the top of the sectional. "This is pretty soft. It'll make a perfect bed for me tonight."

"You are not staying here tonight. It's late, and you're too old to be sleeping on a couch."

"Ouch," Justin said, laughing a bit.

"Yeah, that was rough," Max replied.

"You know what I mean. You should sleep somewhere comfortable, like your own bed."

"She does have several extra bedrooms. I'm sure you

could find a bed that feels just right," Justin said, smiling all the while.

Max sat on the couch. "This one feels just right."

I rolled my eyes obnoxiously. "This isn't the three bears house, and you're definitely not Goldilocks."

He kicked off his shoes and stretched out, lacing his fingers together behind his head. "I am tonight."

I glared at the two men separately. "I'm not going to win this, am I?"

They both shook their heads.

The officer who'd responded to my call approached us. "Ma'am, you said you don't think there's any reason someone would want to steal your computer?"

"I don't see why. There's nothing on it they can use. It's solely a work laptop."

Max sat up.

"Which is exactly why they took it," I said.

"What do you mean?" Justin asked.

I explained what I'd learned, ending with, "This just confuses me more."

"We'll figure it out," Justin said. "In the meantime, I'd like you to step back from talking to anyone else about the pooch parties, okay?"

"But I—"

He raised his hand. "Missy, I'm speaking to you as a police officer, not your daughter's ex-boyfriend."

I nodded. "Yes, sir."

He smiled at Max. "We should be finished up here, but the officer might need you to come to the station tomorrow to go over the details again."

"Yes, sir."

He shook his head and walked toward the front door.

I glanced at Max who was cautiously smiling at me from the couch. I released a loud breath, walked over to the basket on the other side of the sectional, pulled out a blanket and tossed it to him. "The couch or a guest room. Your choice." He stood, removed a gun from the back of his jeans and placed it on the coffee table. "Couch suits me fine, ma'am." He perused the bookcases, grabbing *The Prince* by Niccolo Machiavelli. He held it up toward me. "I'm assuming this was Sam's?"

I nodded. "He felt it taught him a lot, both about what to do and what not to do."

"I've read it. It's a great read for someone wanting to achieve power. It shows the cost that comes with it."

I smiled. "Sam used to say the same thing."

"Great minds."

The police finally left, and after some small talk, Max made himself comfortable on the couch, staring at me as I stood and leaned against the fireplace. "What?"

"It's Jake and Gina. They did this. They've done all of it."

He sat up. "What makes you say that?"

"Collectively, I'm not sure, but individually, a few things, and I just feel like they're in on it together." I rushed to the couch and sat next to him. As I leaned in, I realized we were close enough to touch, and I froze. Max stared into my eyes, and then at my lips, which I swiped the tip of my tongue across because I was nervous. He kept his eyes locked on them for longer than he should, and I scooted myself back, giving us both distance.

I wasn't ready for any of that kind of thing, and I didn't think I'd ever be.

Neither of us acknowledged the moment, but that didn't matter. It happened. It was there, and it would stay there, between us, unacknowledged if I had my way.

"Gina's an opportunist, but not the obvious kind. She's the kind that wants people to think she's not and wants others to root for her. She lets them fake push her into doing things. She did that with me when I suggested she take over the festival. In my defense, it was the obvious choice, but I think she wanted someone to say it so she didn't look like she was being manipulative."

He contemplated that, but I didn't give him enough time to speak.

"And Traci was trying hard to bring Jake down. Not that I disagree with her, but their divorce, from what I heard, was brutal. Everyone knows that. And like I said, I saw him with Gina with his hands on her waist in an intimate way."

Max went to speak, but I kept going, so he just sat and listened.

"Jake's a cheater. Everyone knows that, and he obviously wouldn't want his soon-to-be ex-wife taking him to the cleaners, so what better way to make that happen then to kill her?"

"What does that have to do with Gina Palencia?"

"Two birds, one stone, for lack of a better term anyway. If Jake's sleeping with Gina, he could have manipulated her to kill his wife. Maybe he told her how much money Traci wanted? Maybe they're in love, or maybe she is anyway, and getting rid of Traci gave her both Jake and the head of the festival position."

"What does any of that have to do with the cyanide and vandalism on your turf?"

"It's a distraction. If people are talking about those, and there's a connection, it takes them off Jake and Gina's trail." I nodded, more to myself than to Max. "And it worked. Jake was released from jail, and I've focused on Rick Morring and his efforts to cut the program, not the real killers."

"Listen, like I said before, Jake's not the greatest guy, but I really can't see him as a killer, Missy. I'm sorry."

"He doesn't have an alibi. Not for Traci's murder."

"What do you mean?"

"He claims he was with Gina."

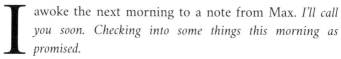

I awoke the next morning to a note from Max. *I'll call you soon. Checking into some things this morning as promised.*

I followed my morning routine, and after I'd let the dogs out one more time, I made the decision to leave them at home instead of bringing them to the fairgrounds. I worried someone might come back and break in, but after thinking it over logically, decided the odds were against it. I just hoped I was right.

There was a last day before the festival volunteer meeting scheduled at nine o'clock, so I headed straight there with a to go mug of coffee from home.

Both Rick and Jake were at the meeting. Neither were volunteers, but Gina didn't seem to mind their attendance. I found it odd. I hadn't had a chance to talk to her about her desire to relocate the pooch party, but since it was the day before the festival, I didn't think she'd have time to swap things around anyway.

"Okay folks, we open tomorrow. I've been reviewing the event map, and after a lot of thought, I've made a decision." Gina focused on me. "Missy, I think the pooch party would be best served at the back of the event."

My mouth dropped. I was wrong. A few volunteers whispered in the crowd.

"I know it's last minute, and I hate to create an issue for you, but I just feel it serves the community best to have them at the back."

"You mean it serves you best," I said.

She blinked. "No, of course not. I just think the dogs are a big draw, and if we put them in the back instead of their current location, everyone that wants to see them will have to go through the entire festival to get to them. It's like saving the best for last."

"Or hiding the worrisome dogs from public eye so they aren't as big of a risk for hurting people."

She flinched, but I couldn't decide if she was honestly surprised by my comment. "No, no. I...I thought it would be a draw that way, Missy. Honestly."

I shook my head. "What are you planning to replace my area with?"

"That's the thing." She smiled as if what she was about to say would make me go along with her plan. She pointed at my not-favorite city council man. "Rick Morring here has suggested a beer garden, and he's already made the necessary permit arrangements to make it happen."

I eyed Max and clenched my fists. "Gina, with all due respect, moving the party location is a lot of work, and I don't know if I can get any of the shelter staff here to help. Besides, I'm not sure it'll work the way you expect."

"I know it would be hard for you, so I've asked a few of the city's crew here to help move it all."

"I think you should—"

She stopped me. "I'm afraid the decision's been made, Missy." She smiled and averted her eyes to Jake Fielding. "Now, up next…"

I stopped listening and stepped away from the crowd for a moment. After I'd gathered my senses and the meeting broke up, I made a beeline straight for Morring.

"This isn't going to happen again, I promise you."

Max stepped next to me and gripped my shoulder. "Missy."

Rick Morring smirked. "I'm not sure what you're implying, Mrs. Kingston."

"Right. But trust me, I'll do whatever's necessary to make

sure my program stays intact. Your fear of dogs aside, this program is a benefit to the community and to the dogs, and I'm not going to let you stop it."

He laughed as he glanced at the small crowd forming around us. "I'm doing no such thing."

I raised my head to the crowd of volunteers, and as I went to speak, Max whispered, "Missy. Let's go."

I narrowed my eyes at him. "No, Max, let's clear up Councilman Morring's concerns right now. What do you think?" I faced the small crowd of volunteers. "Do you all like the pooch parties?"

Several nodded while the rest gave their verbal approval.

"Then please, go to the next city council meeting and say so. Your councilman here is trying to cut the program. He'd rather make money with a beer garden than help families bring love into their lives."

"Will there be additional police here for the beer garden?" A volunteer asked.

"What about the children, Councilman? You're providing an avenue for them to drink illegally. What kind of security will there be?"

"And encouraging people to drink and drive? I shudder at the thought," another person said.

Rick raised his hands. "People, please. Everything has been thought through and every detail attended to. This is a good thing for the community. The money will allow us to do more for others, to provide more opportunities."

"And more cash in your pocket," a man said.

I nodded.

He plastered a fake politician smile on his face. "Give it a try. If you don't like it, then by all means, express that at a council meeting. But for now, the event is already scheduled, and Ms. Palencia is already moving the pooch party to the back of the fairgrounds." He smiled at me. "This is happening, people." He walked away with his shoulders out.

I wanted to scream, but I rushed to the pooch party area to make sure it was handled with care. Max kept up with my pace, trying to calm me the entire way. It didn't work.

Gina Palencia was there, but she wasn't helping them move anything. How could she? Her long skirt and heeled fashionable boots wouldn't fare well hauling things around.

Jake Fielding was there too, dressed in a pair of dark jeans and a nice button down shirt. I glanced at his feet as Jennifer Lee walked up from the inside of the turfed area wearing a pair of black cowboy boots with a pointed toe and thick heel.

Her boots looked like they'd match the prints in my photos perfectly. I glanced at her, my face contorted with a mix of confusion and realization. "Max, I need to go. We'll chat later, okay?"

"Missy, wait," he said.

But I didn't listen. I had to step away and figure out what to do next.

The pooch party area wasn't set up. They'd just moved the turf and threw the crates there haphazardly, and even though I wasn't completely sure Jennifer Lee was responsible for Traci's murder, the festival was coming, and I couldn't let the dogs down. It took me four hours to get everything set back up in the new location. It should have taken more time, but my anger driven adrenaline kept me moving at bionic speed.

When I finished, I sat at my makeshift desk in deep thought. I stared at the ground scanning the dirt area and realizing I'd need to blow off the turf and then spray it down with a hose like I had to every time I prepped for an event.

And that's when I remembered I still had the photos of the boots on my phone. I'd transferred them to my laptop, but they were on the cloud, and I could easily access them, which I did.

I was right, the boot prints could have easily come from Jennifer Lee's boots.

CHAPTER TEN

"I know who killed Traci."

"You what?" Justin breathed quickly. "Where are you?"

"I'm at the pooch party section of the fairgrounds. It's Jennifer. The footprints. I know it. They're hers."

"Stay there. I'm on my way."

I disconnected the call.

"You shouldn't have done that, Missy."

I flipped around and saw Jennifer standing behind me. As I stood, she waved a gun at me and my chair.

"Stay put."

I sat. "Jennifer, I don't...what's going on?" I lied, buying time and hoping Justin would arrive soon.

"I knew you'd figure it out over anyone. You have a way, don't you?"

"A way?"

"Of sticking your nose where it doesn't belong."

"I found Traci by accident, Jennifer. I wasn't out looking for a dead body."

"I'm sure that's exactly what happened with your husband too, wasn't it?"

I flinched.

"Sam this. Sam that. All you do is talk about your dead husband like he was some saint or something. No man is a saint, Missy, that's for sure." She wiggled the gun at me some more. "Take good old Jake Fielding for example. They're all the same."

"Jennifer, listen, we can talk to the police. Get you a good lawyer—"

"A good lawyer? For what, killing a woman that deserved to die? Everyone knew the great, the perfect Traci Fielding was a bitch on wheels. No one even liked her."

"But no one wanted her dead. No one tried to kill her." I grimaced as I'd said that, but it was the truth.

"Because no one had the guts." She pointed the gun at me again. "No one but me."

"This is about Jake isn't it?"

"Well I sure as hell didn't do it because of your stupid dogs." She stared briefly at the turfed area. "Jake tried to get me to push back on your little thing here. Said it would do him a world of good if I could help him get your little party spot *taken care of*, and when I said I wasn't going to try, he dumped me. Moved on to Gina Palencia, and I guess she got the job done."

"What job?"

"What do you think? The beer garden. It's his contract. Why do you think Traci was so against it? She didn't give a crap about your dogs. She just didn't want her husband to profit from the festival."

It all made sense. Jake's businesses. Sports bars. That had to be the company handling the beer garden. How had I missed that connection? "But why kill Traci?"

She laughed. "Why not? The obvious suspect would be

her husband, right? I had the perfect plan to set him up, but you and that nose of yours kept getting in my way. If you'd have just left well enough alone you wouldn't be next on the list."

"Left well enough alone? You tried to poison my dogs."

"It was an unfortunate turn of events, but necessary." She smiled. "For the record, cyanide isn't hard to get."

"Yes, you made that clear before, then tried to act like you didn't."

She narrowed her eyes.

"You wanted Jake and Gina to take the fall, because he's with her and not you. You thought if you vandalized my turf, that would push Gina to move it, and effectively throw both her and Jake under the bus."

She wiggled the gun at me once again. "Bingo, and it was working, too. I listened to the volunteers. They knew about Gina and Jake. People see and they talk. It was perfect."

"But."

She moved closer, the gun maybe a foot from my head. My eyes shifted back and forth. I needed to do something. Justin wasn't there yet and I couldn't hold her off much longer. Where was he?

"But I knew you were digging in, trying to figure out what was happening, and I needed to figure out what you knew."

"That's why you came to my house."

"Of course I did."

"And you're the one that came back and took my computer."

She glanced at her feet and then smiled. "I deleted the pictures of the boot prints. You'll never be able to show them to the police now."

I smiled. "I have the cloud."

She stepped closer, and I had to react. My purse was just

inches away, but I didn't have enough time to grab it and my gun, but I could use what I'd learned in jujitsu. I swung my left arm up, knocking her left arm with my forearm, and sent the gun flying out of her hand. Without pausing, I bowed my head and charged her from the seat, forcing her to fall back onto the ground, smacking her head onto the hard Georgia dirt. It caught her off guard, and for a moment she lay there disoriented. I pushed her out of my way and threw myself at the gun, landing with my chest on top of it. I rolled over and grabbed it with my dominate hand just in time to roll over again and point it at Jennifer Lee standing above me. As she bent down, I lifted my leg and kicked her in the knee, and I heard something crack.

She screamed as she fell back again, rolling to her side and cursing loudly. She stood and rushed toward me again. I pushed myself up off the ground and pointed the gun at her, but she kept coming. I didn't want to shoot her. She may have been a killer, but I wasn't. I threw the gun over her head and it sailed through the air, landing several feet behind her and stood with my feet slightly separated, my hands in fists protecting my face.

She stopped and growled, "You son of a b—"

"Cursing isn't ladylike," I said and threw a jab at her face with one hand. When it surprised her, I grabbed a handful of her hair and yanked her back down to the ground. "And I've learned that where the head goes, the body follows."

She screamed out as she dropped on her injured leg just as Justin and Detective Bruno arrived, guns drawn. I kept at it, throwing myself on top of Jennifer to keep her from going anywhere. Later, I'd learn I'd broken her leg with that kick, and it was unlikely she could have stood on it again.

"Missy, stop. We got this."

Max met me at the police station. I'd already given my statement to Bruno and Justin, but they weren't ready to let me go home. Max talked with them both, privately, and after he finished, he sat with me in the private lounge the officers used. "Jake wanted Jennifer to kill his wife."

"I had a feeling."

"And when she refused, when she wouldn't help him with his mission or whatever he called it, he enlisted Gina Palencia."

"Yes."

"So, Jennifer did it anyway, trying to frame them."

"You're not telling me anything I don't already know," I said.

"I was wrong."

"About what?"

"Jake Fielding is a killer."

I nodded. "Just not one that wanted to get blood on his hands. Literally."

He held my hand in his. "I'm sorry."

"About what?"

"About not protecting you. I made a promise to Sam and I didn't follow through. In fact, I did the opposite by asking you to help a friend who ended up wanting to kill someone. I'm—"

I turned and faced him. "Max, stop. You're wrong. This was personal for me, and Sam would know that. I know that. You didn't make me do anything. It started with me finding the body."

He half-smiled. "I should have done something."

"You did. You stayed on my couch. You kept me safe. Sam would appreciate that. I appreciate that."

He nodded. "Thank you for that, but I still feel like I let you both down."

I smiled as I squeezed his hand. "I know Sam, and I promise you, you haven't, neither of us."

Justin knocked on the door and stepped into the small lounge. "We have Gina. She's admitted to her part in Jake's plan. Said he tried to get her to push Traci out, and told her if that meant his wife had to die, he was okay with that."

"Is she under arrest?"

He shook his head. "But we've got someone picking up Fielding now."

I exhaled. "That's good."

"You need to go home." He squeezed my shoulder. "And you need to call your daughter."

"I will, but I really need to—"

"No, Missy. She knows. She's waiting to hear from you."

But I didn't need to call Hayden. Her car was in my driveway when Max pulled in.

"I can stay," he said.

I shook my head. "It's okay. She's harmless, for the most part anyway."

He smiled. "I'll call you later?"

I nodded, and we both stared at each other again, our eyes locking with that awkward desire I wasn't ready or willing to acknowledge. I looked away and said goodbye as I stepped out of his car.

Hayden hugged me and cried.

That night she slept in my room with me. The night Sam died, she stayed in my bed, too. We both cried each other to sleep then, and in some odd way, I think it made us both feel better, or maybe just feel less alone. I was grateful she was there, but I knew it was more for her than for me. I'd already lost my husband. Being close to death didn't scare me, but I knew the thought of me dying scared Hayden.

The next morning, I got up extra early to get to the shelter and organize the dogs to head out to the festival. I was grateful Hayden had come over again because Max had driven me to the police station the night before and I'd left my car at the fairgrounds.

When we arrived at the festival, hours before it was to start, I groaned about the long walk to the back of the fairgrounds to the pooch party area. As we walked, Gina Palencia stepped out of a specialty hot chocolate booth.

"Missy."

I stiffened at the sound of her voice.

"Gina."

She touched her lips. "Your…the…if you're going to your area, you need to turn around."

"What do you mean?"

"Several of the volunteers moved it back to its original location." She shrugged. "I thought it was the least I could do."

I nodded. "What about the beer garden?"

"It's back there. Drives foot traffic through the whole festival." She smiled. "I'm…I'm sorry."

Hayden grabbed my arm. "Mom, we have things to do."

"One minute," I said, and steeled my eyes on Gina. "Are you? I could have been killed."

"I know that now. I didn't think any of this would happen."

"Can I ask you a question?"

She nodded.

"Do you love him?"

"I thought I might. I don't know now."

"Next time you might want to choose better."
Hayden coughed.
"Yes," Gina said.
We walked away.
"You just owned her, Mom."
I smiled. "I like to think I was giving her valuable advice."
"As you owned her."

CHAPTER ELEVEN

The pooch party was a hit. We had training sessions every hour on the hour, showing off the dog's skills while allowing potential adopters to engage with the dogs through mini training and play. Hours into the first night, Hayden showed up with a familiar person holding her hand.

Justin blushed. "How're you feeling Mrs.—Missy?"

"Apparently not as happy as you." I couldn't help myself, mostly because I was just as happy to see them holding hands as I knew he was.

"Mom."

"What? This is a dream come true for me."

Hayden smiled and pushed her shoulder into Justin's. "I kind of feel that way, too."

"Your father would be thrilled."

We all stood there thinking about Sam and what he would have felt in that moment.

As we made small talk, Mary from the shelter signed the papers for another adoption process. In all that first night, we had four applications for adoption. I considered that a success.

When Rick Morring approached the pooch party area with his wife and two children, I had to force myself to be kind to the man. While his wife supervised his children playing with the dogs, he approached me.

"This isn't over, Mrs. Kingston."

I adjusted the collar on one of the dog's necks and stood. "I have no doubt about that, Mr. Morring. I mean, look at them." I flicked my head toward his children, smiling as his daughter, who wasn't over seven years old, was attacked with kisses by Allie. "They're so dangerous." His family laughed as the children rolled around with the pups on the ground. Allie was in heaven.

Rick Morring shook his head and called out to his wife. "Come on, babe, let's get these kids some funnel cake." He nodded at me. "Mrs. Kingston."

I gave him a snarky smile, but that was it.

Allie and Bandit fascinated visitors by playing together with their *Kong* as a volunteer trainer tossed it around. That trainer approached me as the festival ended that first night.

Her face full of worry, she whispered in my ear, "Mrs. Kingston, someone wants to adopt Bandit."

I pushed myself from my kneeling position. "Bandit?"

She nodded. "Yes, ma'am." She aimed her eyes toward a red-haired woman sitting at the table with the adoption applications. "What should I tell her?"

I smiled. "I'll take care of it, sweetie. Can you do me a favor and start walking the dogs to the shelter van?"

"Yes, ma'am."

I ambled over to the desk and greeted the woman. "I understand you're interested in adopting a dog?"

She smiled. "Yes, I'd like to adopt that black one, Bandit. Though I'd definitely have to change that name."

I pressed my lips together. "We received an application for him already, and I suspect they'll be approved. We could contact you, or you could consider another dog?" I didn't tell her that other application was mine just waiting to be signed.

"Oh, that's too bad, but I did love that little Corgi mix. It looks just like a Husky, but with a Corgi body. I noticed another couple with her though. Is she being adopted?"

I pulled an application from the file folder to my right. "No, ma'am. Willie is available. Go ahead and fill this out, and we'll start the interview process tomorrow."

After she completed the application and left, I finished the last of the items on my closing list and hugged Bandit. "First thing in the morning Monday we're signing those adoption papers. Time to make it official."

I was exhausted, but we'd got everything set up for the next day, and I could finally go home and fall into bed.

Max met me at my car.

"Oh, hey. It's late. What're you still doing here?" I asked.

"Figured I'd stick around and make sure you got home okay."

I smiled. "Max, thank you, but really, I'm fine." I loaded the dogs into my car and checked to make sure the shelter van had already left. I was relieved to see it had. After I closed the door, I started my vehicle with my key and popped open my door to roll the windows down for the dogs.

"Missy, I..." He shifted his body weight from one leg to the other and ran a hand through his short hair. He smiled, and my breath quickened.

"Max, I think I know what you're going to—"

He stepped closer and I froze. I couldn't look at him, couldn't lift my eyes from his chest to his face, but that didn't matter. He used one finger and lifted my chin for me. "You feel it too, don't you?"

I licked my lips.

"I really want to kiss you, you know that?"

I wasn't sure what to say, which didn't matter because I don't think my voice could have made it past the huge lump in my throat. "Max, I…I can't."

He smiled as he removed his finger and stepped back a step. "I understand." He glanced at the ground and then up at me again. "You'll get home okay?"

I blinked. "I'll be fine."

"I'll follow you just in case."

"Max, you don't have to do—"

"Sam would want me to. And Missy, he'd want you to be happy." Before I could say anything, he continued. "I can wait."

"I don't know if I'll ever be ready, Max."

"Maybe not, but you'll always have me looking out for you."

ACKNOWLEDGMENTS

Thank you to my wonderful editor, Jen, my favorite proofreader, JC Wing, ARC supervisor and assistant, Wilfrieda Schultz for keeping me in line, my wonderful ARC team, and my friends and family who've supported me as I've traveled along this writing journey. Most of all, thank you to my *Hottie Hubby* for being my best friend and my biggest fan.

ABOUT THE AUTHOR

Even though I've always wanted to be a writer, I also wanted to support myself, so instead of following that dream, I opted to get a job with a regular paycheck.

When my mother died in 2009, and then I lost my father less than a year later, I decided to take the leap. I wanted to find a way to honor my parents, to keep their memories alive, and I did that with my first book, Unfinished Business.

That book went to number one all over and sat happily in the top one hundred books sold in each for over a week with one particular outlet.

I received hundreds of emails from people who felt that little semi-mystery gave them hope, that it made them find comfort when they needed it most, and that they wished they had a friend like Mel.

I was hooked.

I don't write for the money (though the money is nice

sometimes). I write for those emails, and knowing I'm doing what I love, finally. If my writing takes people away from their worries for even a short period of time, I'm a lucky gal.

I hope my parents can read in Heaven.

Join my mailing list here.
Follow me on Facebook

OTHER BOOKS BY CAROLYN RIDDER ASPENSON

The Angela Panther Mystery Series

Unfinished Business

Unbreakable Bonds

Uncharted Territory

Unexpected Outcomes

Unbinding Love

The Christmas Elf

The Ghosts

Undetermined Events

The Event

The Favor

The Lily Sprayberry Realtor Cozy Mystery Series

Deal Gone Dead

Decluttered and Dead

The Scarecrow Snuff Out (in Sleigh Bells & Sleuthing, a holiday novella collection)

Signed, Sealed and Dead

Bidding War Break-In

Open House Heist

Realtor Rub Out

Santa's Little Thief (in the 12 Cozy Mystery Carols of Christmas)

Foreclosure Fatality (coming soon)

The Chantilly Adair Psychic Medium Cozy Mystery Series

Get Up and Ghost

Ghosts Are People Too

Praying for Peace

Haunting Hooligans

Ghost in the Grave (coming soon)

The Pooch Party Cozy Mystery Series

Pooches, Pumpkins, and Poison

Hounds, Harvest, and Homicide (coming soon)

The Holiday Hills Witch Cozy Mystery Series

There's a New Witch in Town (coming soon)

AUTHORS NEED LOVE!

If you enjoyed this book then I'd really appreciate it if you would post a short review where you purchased your copy. Reviews help authors grow as writers and help other readers find our books.

Please keep in touch with me through my newsletter at carolynridderaspenson.com

Made in the
USA
Columbia, SC